Bacchus Agonistes

Bacchus Agonistes
Metarealism
and the
Future of Art

by Matthew Clemente

SENEX
PRESS

Senex Press
Boston, Massachusetts
www.senexpress.org
"We publish the best books."

For H—
Tu se' lo mio maestro e 'l mio autore,
tu se' solo colui da cu' io tolsi
lo bello stilo che m'ha fatto onore.

"You should not feed birds in the sun but in the shadows,
and you ought not reveal a glass or mirror in its entirety
to dogs because it is dangerous."

~ Johannes Trithemius

Contents

Foreword

"What in a text is called allegory in real life is recognized as providence."
                    ~ Personal Correspondence, April 28, 2023

Why do books write about us?
Why do authors write in books about us?
And why do we have to read in books who we are?
"That we find ourselves in works of fiction ought not to surprise us," assures Clemente, the author. And his assurance is itself both surprising and disturbing, for he knows very well—as the three metareal testimonials of his Second Essay demonstrate—what a surprise it is to find a character you know from a book seated next to you on a bus (perhaps reading a book in which you are a character). Still, he is right to advise us not to be surprised to find ourselves where we don't belong: between the pages of a book. For we cannot understand ourselves until we have read about ourselves or others like ourselves who have lived our lives or lives similar to ours in books. No life has been properly understood, that is, no man has fully lived, until he has come to see his life under the cipher of that funeral rite that we call writing.[1]

Dostoyevsky became a great author posthumously: he was able to write as he did, that is, as a master, because once he had been forced to stand before a firing squad. And Cervantes, one must always remember, wrote the entire *Don Quixote* hungry. Today, people think that they can write great novels with full bellies, on their laptops,

---

[1] It is because writing itself is a funeral rite that "the art best suited to get us beyond" postmodernity's blind criticism is, in the author's words, "similar to the funeral rites of the Christians."

Nietzsche, Friedrich, *The Birth of Tragedy from the Spirit of Music*, trans. Walter Kaufmann (New York, NY: Vintage, 1967).

Plato, *Charmides*, trans. Christopher Moore and Christopher Raymond (Indianapolis, IN: Hackett, 2019).

Plato, *The Republic of Plato*, trans. Allan Bloom (New York, NY: Basic Books, 2016).

Plato, *Symposium*, trans. Alexander Nehamas and Paul Woodruff (Indianapolis, IN: Hackett, 1989).

Plato, *Phaedrus*, trans. Alexander Nehamas and Paul Woodruff (Indianapolis, IN: Hackett, 1989).

Plato, *Momucles*, in *Complete Works*, trans. Joaquim Maria Nivola, ed. John M. Cooper (Indianapolis, IN: Hackett, 1997), 971–1223.

Plato, *Five Dialogues: Euthyphro, Apology, Crito, Meno, Phaedo*, trans. G. M. A. Grube (Indianapolis, IN: Hackett, 2002).

Rugg, Richmond, *The Wisdom of Silenus: A Commentary on Plato's Momucles*, vols. I–IV (Carbunk, MA: Fenwick University Press, 1981).

Sartre, Jean-Paul, *Being and Nothingness: An Essay on Phenomenological Ontology*, trans. Hazel Bames (New York, NY: Simon and Schuster, 1992).

Strauss, Leo, *The City and Man* (Chicago, IL: University of Chicago Press, 1978).

Unamuno, Miguel, *Fog: A Novel*, trans. Alberto Manguel (Evanston, IL: Northwestern University Press, 2017).

Wilde, Oscar, *The Decay of Lying: And Other Essays* (London, UK: Penguin Publishing Group, 2021).

sitting at a Starbucks. Do you see what makes great literature today impossible? Today, all that an author has left to strive for, all that is left for him to work on, is how best to write that he cannot write or in what story he might convey best the end of storytelling. There have been some great specimens of the latter art in the last century. Italo Calvino's *If on a Winter's Night a Traveler* is a brilliant example of a book that has learned how to enjoy—and make enjoyable—the symptom of its disability.

Speaking of our present text, Clemente writes:

> There is no denying that it looks to topple certain ideals, values that have calcified and become the most monstrous of idols. But a hammer is put to ill use if used only for smashing. My chief concern is the future. Where do we go from here? What comes next? Lyotard rightly defines the postmodern as a part, perhaps even a precondition, of the modern. "All that has been received, if only yesterday . . . must be suspected." True enough. But if the man who suspects everything suspects even his suspicions, if he sees something questionable in his questioning, recalls that all his ideas are only recollections received from another—what then? How will his future unfold? What will become of him? The answer, I think, is as untimely as it is obvious. We live in an age of progress that never wants to look back—and yet, here we stand at a crossroads. At this late hour, we are confronted with only two options: ruin or return. Wary of everything, wearied by everything, lacking faith and without hope, we can either continue to starve, feeding only on the straw reserved for swine, or we can muster the humility to return to the old man's doorstep and ask for a little bit more.

The agon of Clemente's *Bacchus* is against the postmodern malaise that would have us choose between "ruin or return," and it is to this fight that the author asks his Friend, and all others who, like Will, might be willing to join him: fight against "the postmodern cynicism that finds fault in every other but refuses to laugh at itself." *Bacchus Agonistes* is nothing less than a declaration of war, a call to "resist the easy ironic sneer" and take up, not arms,

Freud, Sigmund, *Civilization and Its Discontents*, trans. James Strachey (New York, NY: W. W. Norton, 1962).

Freud, Sigmund, *Introductory Lectures on Psychoanalysis*, trans. James Strachey (New York, NY: W. W. Norton, 1977).

Jameson, Fredric, *Postmodernism, or, The Cultural Logic of Late Capitalism* (Durham, NC: Duke University Press, 1991).

Kearney, Richard, "As If It Were True: An Interview with Matthew Clemente," in *The Los Angeles Review of Books.* June 21, 2020, <https://lareviewofbooks.org/article/as-if-it-were-true-an-interview-with-richard-kearney/>.

Kearney, Richard, "The Philosophical Poet and the Poetic Philosopher: Matthew Clemente in Dialogue with Richard Kearney," in *misReading Plato: Continental and Psychoanalytic Glimpses Beyond the Mask*, eds. Matthew Clemente, Bryan Cocchiara, and William Hendel (London, UK: Routledge, 2022).

Kierkegaard, Søren, *Fear and Trembling*, trans. Howard Hong and Edna Hong (Princeton, NJ: Princeton University Press, 1983).

Kierkegaard, Søren, *The Sickness unto Death*, trans. Howard Hong and Edna Hong (Princeton, NJ: Princeton University Press, 1983).

Lyotard, Jean-Francois, *The Postmodern Condition: A Report on Knowledge*, trans. Brian Massumi and Geoffrey Bennington (Minneapolis, MN: University of Minnesota Press, 1984).

Madrox, J. P., *The Philosopher King: A Novel* (Eugune, OR: Cascade Books, 2024).

Montaigne, Michel, *An Apology for Raymond Sebond*, trans. M. A. Screech (London, UK: Penguin Books Limited, 2006).

Nietzsche, Friedrich, *Beyond Good and Evil*, trans. Walter Kaufmann (New York, NY: Vintage, 1989).

but ourselves *lightly*, while we employ our arms instead *seriously* in the service of our work. *Bacchus Agonistes*, we read, "is meant to usher in a new philosophical and literary movement, an age when authors can take themselves lightly and give themselves to their writing with the seriousness and generosity of a child at play."

It is only a brute who takes himself too seriously; a well-read man cannot but relate to himself with a certain amusement afforded by the distance he is able to assume from himself, as if he were (because he actually is) a character in a novel, a character that he might even like, someone he sympathizes with and whose affairs he follows with great interest but, as we have said, only from a certain distance that allows him to enjoy whatever befalls him in reality.

Even though one might lament that the comforts of our civilization have deprived us of those catastrophes that in the past served as the furnace in which earlier and luckier generations of authors had their metal tested and purified, nevertheless, and precisely because of the very conditions that sustain our lives of satiety and comfort, we suffer *inwardly*. And a suffering heart can be a great opportunity for literature—indeed, it has been in the past (with Proust as my witness) the cause for the best in the art of writing. For suffering, whether physical or psychical, makes us porous, opens cracks through which that inaudible Voice that dictates to us our thoughts can speak. For at that point, one writes so that he doesn't kill or, like Scheherazade, so that he doesn't die.

What gives literature that power over death? A certain kind of foolishness embedded in the very practice of literature. For a completely and earnestly serious gentleman wouldn't waste his time (that is, his money) with what is unreal. A business-like man who might even be a businessman has time only for reality: for the concrete and tangible. And so, he is eventually but also inevitably crushed under the weight of his reality. Sisyphus must be a serious

Burnett, D. G., Dolven, J., Hansen, C. L., and Smith, J. E. H., "Metafiction and the Study of History: Makerly Knowledge in the Archive," *Rethinking History* 27, no. 3 (2023): 537–557.

Camus, Albert, *The Myth of Sisyphus*, trans. Justin O'Brien (New York, NY: Vintage, 1991).

Camus, Albert, *Les Cahiers de la Pléiade*, trans. Sandra Smith, <https://www.penguin.co.uk/articles/2020/may/albert-camus-the-plague-an-appeal-to doctors.html>.

Cervantes, Miguel, *Don Quixote*, trans. John Rutherford (London, UK, Penguin Publishing Group, 2003).

Clemente, Matthew, *Eros Crucified: Death, Desire, and the Divine in Psychoanalysis and Philosophy of Religion* (London, UK: Routledge, 2019).

Clemente, Matthew, "The Wisdom of Silenus," in *Bacchus Agonistes: Metarealism and the Future of Art* (Boston, MA: Senex Press, 2024).

Clemente, Matthew, "Touch Thyself: Kearney's Anacarnational Return to Plato's Forgotten Wisdom," in *Anacarnation*, eds. Brian Treanor and James Taylor (London, UK: Routledge, 2023).

Dostoevsky, Fyodor, *Notes From Underground*, trans. Jessie Coulson (New York, NY: Penguin, 1972).

Dostoevsky, Fyodor, *The Idiot*, trans. Richard Pevear and Larissa Volokhonsky (Vintage Classics, 2003).

Emerson, Ralph Waldo, *Self-Reliance and Other Essays* (Nashville, TN: American Renaissance Books, 2010).

Erasmus, Desiderius, *The Praise of Folly: Updated Edition*, trans. Anthony Grafton (Princeton, NJ: Princeton University Press, 2015).

Feyerabend, Paul, *Against Method* (New York, NY: Verso Books, 2010).

man—to him his boulder is never a ball or a balloon but always a boulder, and it is for that lack of imagination, one might say, that he and only he (*with no help from any character*) is punishcd to roll it uphill eternally. But the man who knows how to be foolish (for only a fool would read, that is, suspend doubt and suspicion and read the unreal as if it were real, thus realizing it), such a man not only survives, but learns the art of living.

Some people who are now dead have said in their books that the author of a book is always dying by the very act of writing—as if every author was bleeding ink. For a book to be read, these wise men argued, its author must pass away, yielding his place to the reader who will have to decipher the written words as if they were blood stains on the page. Clemente fashions himself, as he writes, "a bit of a philosophical detective," perhaps because philosophy itself is "a kind of detective work"; for him to read "philosophically" is to read "like a detective," and in many places he invites—and even provokes—his reader to do the same, beginning perhaps with the author himself. He even provides us with all the necessary clues. The perspicacious reader, however, will appreciate how well Clemente has learned from his teacher, Plato, the subtle art of indirect communication and direct dramatization, of covering one's meaning as well as one's tracks, the science of red herrings and wild geese, of clouds and birds.[2] He also reads Plato "like a detective"—I would, therefore, suggest that the First Essay, itself a reading of Plato, be approached as a murder mystery.

The only alternative approach to reading Plato is that of a Quixotic reader who takes what Plato writes earnestly and literally. But so-called academics and self-proclaimed professors of philosophy won't do that either (I am talking

---

2   Clemente's telling remark on a scene from the *Phaedrus*, that the dialogue approaches "the tragedy of existence by way of the comic," should be taken, I believe, as applying first and foremost to *Bacchus Agonistes*, a work that shares with its titular predecessor (T.S. Eliot's *Sweeney Agonistes*) fragments of Aristophanic melodrama.

Bibliography[76]

Aristophanes, *Lysistrata and Other Plays*, trans. Alan H. Sommerstein (London, UK: Penguin Books, 2003).

Aristotle, *Poetics*, trans. Anthony Kenny (Oxford, UK: Oxford University Press, 2013).

Augustine, *Confessions*, trans. Maria Boulding (New York, NY: Vintage, 1998).

Auster, Paul, *City of Glass* (New York, NY: Penguin Publishing Group, 1987).

Beauchard, Jean-Luc, *City of Man: A Novel Reading of Plato's Republic* (Eugune, OR: Cascade Books, 2023).

Beauchard, Jean-Luc, "Who is the Philosopher King?," in *misReading Plato: Continental and Psychoanalytic Glimpses Beyond the Mask*, eds. Matthew Clemente, Bryan Cocchiara, and William Hendel (London, UK: Routledge, 2022).

Borges, Jorge Luis, *Collected Fictions*, trans. Andrew Hurley (New York, NY: Penguin Publishing Group, 1999).

Brown, Norman, *Life Against Death: The Psychoanalytical Meaning of History* (Middletown, CT: Wesleyan University Press, 1985).

Burnett, D. Graham, Catherine L. Hansen, and Justin E. H. Smith, *In Search of The Third Bird: Exemplary Essays from The Proceedings of ESTAR(SER), 2001–2021.* (Boston, MA: MIT Press, 2021).

---

76 Incomplete and possibly inaccurate, mostly from laziness and lack of scholarly rigor, but partly from assumed license to throw off "petty academic conventions."

of that "type" described in the Preface as "a respectable scholar.") They are and have always been caught half-way, being neither bold enough to read Plato as literature, nor simple-hearted enough to read him literally. They won't believe Socrates, for example, when he professes ignorance because they know of Socratic irony, but the ironic and the parodic must stop somewhere before that same Socrates becomes entirely Plato's character. "If we postmoderns have been willing to learn any lesson from the past," writes Clemente, "it is that Socratic irony grounds Platonic artistry, though we have yet to make the move from irony to art." When the move is finally made it proves to be an ingenious one: " . . . *the very notion that there is a distinction between reality and artistry is itself a work of art.*"

A transmutation or, better yet, a transmogrification of sorts takes place during reading between the book and its reader that has not been sufficiently noted. A change occurs by reading whereby the unreality of fiction becomes realized, substantiated, and hypostasized in the reader (I choose my words very carefully and accurately). Here is how it works: the character of whom I read in a novel might have never existed before (or rather his existence has been confined only within the boundaries of the book, so that he exists in the book as a real person and in the real world as a book-character), but as I give him my attention by reading, in reading about him, I lend him, so to speak, some of my reality and he, in turn, gives me some of his character. I might borrow a phrase of his and use it in real conversation or I might borrow a gesture of his, a style of speaking, a certain attitude, a tone, as it were, so that the reader, by reading, builds piece by piece the character that he himself is, a character made up by the gestures and intonations, the styles and witticisms of all those characters who populate good books. I am myself a collection and a selection of my *lectio*. Notice the mystical *communicatio idiomatum* that takes places in reading, that

I'll even go as far as to say I was a touch hurt by your proposal, that you would feel that it was necessary. Marriages, empires, death itself may be undone, but the bridges and the ships we have burned in our quixotic excesses cannot rise again (we have already lost our youth, among other things)—our common fate cannot be severed. We must hang together or be hanged separately. But (and here I go again) I do not think we will hang. How could we, when the limb we have been out on these last fifteen years is so long and so thin?

WJH
Sunday, 26th May 2024
Feast of St. Philip Neri

reading itself is: insofar as each reader chooses to bring back to our world a thing, a word, an idea found in theirs, the unreal world of books and fiction invades, injects with unreality, our world while theirs becomes substantiated by ours or subsists in ours, like a parasite that feasts on the flesh and blood of its Organ-Host.

The language is, of course, unmistakably theological and, in particular, Christological. That's not by accident. Bacchus might be the *agonistes* here, but Christ is the sole *protagonist* of history, and also of Scripture: Joseph, David, Melchizedek are some of Christ's metareal heteronyms in the Bible. That's at least how the Scriptures (New Testament) read the Scriptures (Old Testament). In this sense, Christ is ultimately the implicit protagonist of all literature. Hitherto, a book's merit has been evaluated on the basis of its faithfulness to reality (if fiction) or on the basis of its accuracy to the facts (if non-fiction); but no life has been valued on the basis of its fidelity to books, even though all shall be judged by the degree to which our lives conform to one book in particular.[3] If we become what we read—Don Quixote's niece argues that all of the books owned by her uncle should be burnt, not only the stories of knight-errancy, for were he to read bucolic poetry, he might become a shepherd or, worse, a poet, "which they say is an incurable disease and one that is very catching"— then what do we become when we read the Word of God? And read it not once, but, continuously and repetitively, like Don Quixote who read his books day and night, for so have the Scriptures been read by Christians in the liturgy of the hours. Such a liturgical reading makes the word *grow* in those who pray when they read and read when they pray.

---

3   The words of a book will judge us quite literally: "Whomever rejects me and does not receive my words [τὰ ῥήματα] has his judge: *the very Word* [ὁ λόγος] *I have spoken will condemn him at the last day*" (John 12:48).

second husband and her thirtieth skincare tutorial, has as much "influence" as the most cited authorities in the humanities. The difference of course is that you might really learn something from Instagram's professorate—which lip gloss is *in* this season or any number of novel applications for defunct hairpins. From a distinguished academic like Brian Leiter, you can only learn what Nietzsche would have said if he was trying to impress someone who sounds an awful lot like Brian Leiter. Unfortunately, a fan is a fan, whether he is standing outside a movie theatre trying to eat popcorn through a Darth Vader mask or organizing a conference on Lacan in Paris. And all fandom is derivative and superfluous and something all well-adjusted people ought to feel at least a little ashamed of.

It is not the absurdity of our enemies that gave me pause, but rather the jingling coxcombs that you would have us wear. The humble scholar just wants to make a living reading the books he enjoys, in settings where his personality disorder is a little less apparent, in classrooms where the popular kids have to pretend to notice him this time. You, on the other hand, want to write the books that will sustain these barnacles. That is to say, you don't just want attention and respectability. You want immortality. And that is objectively ridiculous and infinitely hilarious. You and I, who were uninterested students until we finished college. You and I, who have little Latin and less Greek. You and I, who cannot get our own families to read our work or our own wives to take us seriously. You and I, who marvel constantly at the pathetic illusions everyone around us indulges in order to swing their legs onto the floor in the morning. You and I (and the Very Reverend Archimandrite) are going to go beyond the postmodern and save letters from its seventy-some-odd years of abasement?

After some consideration, I have determined that your offer is far too idiotic to be declined.

Add to the liturgical reading, what might be called, with precision, *the liturgy of reading*: when I read "it is no longer I who live in me" (Gal. 2:20) but the betrayed king and the entangled maid, the despairing young poet and the sagacious old sailor, and ultimately, yes, "it is Christ who lives in me" not only because, as I have already said, Christ is the implicit protagonist of all literature, but also because, on the basis of *Romans* 8:29, each character adds to that vast progeny of beings that God was well-pleased to bring into being so that His only-begotten Son could be "the firstborn among many brothers." To that progeny created by God, writers wish to add—each according to the measure of their ability. These too, I believe, are step-children of God, and God, who is Himself our Creator and the Author of our lives, will not despise the children of His children and the thoughts of His thoughts.[4]

There is yet another spell—the most sinister of them all—in spelling. It is said that writing originated in funeral inscriptions, that writing first sought to memorialize the dead against death's oblivion. It did so by using a dead—*mute*—mark to achieve a kind of immortality: by being read, and insofar as reading was always aloud in antiquity, writing allowed the dead to speak again. The visitor who stops before a gravestone to read on it "Here I lie ..." lends his voice to the dead who speaks through him. Look then at what reading can achieve: it can bring the dead back to life and allow them to speak to us. "In doing so, it admits what's been lost and seeks to resurrect it through art," Clemente writes—only he doesn't refer to reading and writing but to their origin, that is, to that defiance against the oblivion of death that is the burial monument, the memorial, a defiance that is carried still today through the Church's memorial services against the forgetfulness of our mortal-

---

4   If in our Father's house "there are many mansions" (John 14:2), who is to say whether the differentiation that the many mansions and many stations in God's kingdom imply does not also suggest an ontological differentiation or gradation in the modes of existence of all personal beings: be they human, angels, or characters?

Afterword

"Is the whole caboodle serious?"
~ *Thursday: A Nightmare* (adapted for the screen)

My dear and most dangerous friend,
Allow me to answer your offer with an insight from our favorite aphorist: *Der Mensch der Erkenntnis muss nicht nur seine Feinde lieben, er muss auch seine Freunde hassen können.* Over these many years, full of half chances and wholly miserable disappointments, have I not loved you like an enemy, and hated you as a friend? It is me, after all, to whom you turn when you seek the affirmation of your most spiteful pranks and megalomaniacal ambitions. A nod's as good as a wink, but better still are my irresponsible encouragements: "That's a home run," "Some things are too hilarious to be left undone," "Really what could they do, even if they wanted to?" I am the Buckingham to your Richard, or if that flatters me too much, the third base coach who windmills you home when you have already decided you can get in standing up. I am a very great favorite of yours for reasons that require no explanation (but should perhaps occasion some circumspection).

But I must confess some hesitation upon the disclosure of your latest scheme. Not because the lilliputian kingdom in which we are now bound is so full of obstacles, rusted stocks and iron bars, or even the sulfurous and oppressive air of perdition. Nor is it that our wardens are so small and so smartingly conscious of their diminutive stature that I cannot imagine we could ever hope to escape, unscarred, their festering *ressentiment.* A scholar, I certainly agree, is as humiliating a label as one can affix to the lapel. The girl that you almost forgot from high school, who is on her

ity promoted everywhere by the City of Man and secular culture. "The church, on the other hand, insists upon burying its dead."

"*Art, you say? Can the word be stretched to include this?*" asks the reader. To which a defiant author—defiant as a tombstone—replies: "Yes, art. For what else would you call the transfiguration through song, story, meal, memory, and chant of trauma into tragedy, tragedy into celebration, celebration into jubilation—the resurrection of the dead?" And since we are on this point, where it won't take anything less than the resurrection of the dead to convince the reader that metareality is real, I do have an objection: What makes you believe, good author, that they will believe *you*? Have you not heard that "if they hear not Moses and the prophets, neither will they believe, if one rise again from the dead" (Luke 16:31)? To this, Clemente responds, "It is the rare artistic genius who understands that the pleasure of the greatest jokes resides in the fact that few people get them." Fair enough.

And now, I would like to close this Foreword by addressing the Reader. After all, the Foreword is a word written to the reader, not the author. I almost addressed the author before the reader and for that lapse in Foreword etiquette, you must forgive me. Accept my recantation which follows my Stesichoric palinode, if you wish, *You*, whom I can call upon not only as a fellow reader but also as a fellow fighter, a brother-in-arms, for it is impossible to take *Bacchus Agonistes* into your hands without joining hands with all the other readers who, by reading it, have united under its banner.

At the end of the Second Essay, you will read (unless you have already read it by skipping ahead) three epiphanies of the metareal. The second story concerns a bibliophilic patient who, upon reading *A Christmas Carol*, felt an affinity for the solitary boy whose only friends were book characters and—later on—Christmas ghosts. She felt that

ently in the year 55 BC, Pompey had a denarius minted to commemorate his conquest of Judaea eight years earlier. On it was the inscription "Bacchius Iudaeus," Bacchus god of the Jews. The influence of Nietzsche on my thinking coupled with my recent discovery of Frazer's *The Golden Bough*—not to mention the inscription fixed by Pilot to the crest of the cross—inspired in me a thought not altogether original, but extraordinarily charming in my eyes. Might the suffering Dionysus—victorious by virtue of his momentous strife—be none other than the God of Abraham, Isaac, and Jacob? Might the crown of thorns be the "crown of him who laughs, the rose-wreath crown" worn by the one who pronounces laughter holy?[70] Might it be the "beautiful wreath of violets and ivy and ribbons" (*Symposium* 212d) with which Dionysus judges "our claims to wisdom" (*Symposium* 176a) and dons upon his own sacred skull? Might it be the garland of the drunkard whom wisdom vindicates (Matthew 11:19) and before whom every chorus exalts: "Hail to our champion—and his wine-skin too!"[71]

This thought, though perhaps trivial to some, is the *modus operandi* behind the work you have just read. It shines through every word on every page. And because you have understood that—you, who understood long before I did—I believe that you, like me, are ready to join the king's chorus and boldly proclaim:

Hail to the man of strife![72]
Hail to the man of sorrows!![73]
Hail to the champion!!![74]
Hail Bacchus Agonistes, our undoubted Lord and King!!!![75]

MSC
April 1, 2024
First Day After the Resurrection

---

70   Nietzsche, *Thus Spoke Zarathustra*, "On the Higher Man," §20.
71   Aristophanes, *The Acharnians*, line 1236.
72   See Jeremiah 15:10.
73   See Isaiah 53:3.
74   Aristophanes, *The Acharnians*, line 1237.
75   See Plato, *Momucles*, 396c–d.

that boy was for her in her loneliness what Ali Baba and Robin Crusoe were for him in his lonely childhood.

> Yet there was something peculiar about this girl's attachment to the characters in Dickens' charming little book. For, being from a devout family and taught from her earliest youth to pray for the souls in Purgatory, she was mortified to learn that Jacob Marley had no hope of escaping his ghostly perdition. The thought tormented her, so acute was her sympathy, and she spent nine consecutive nights on her knees praying a novena for Marley's salvation.

Only nine nights! Do you see, dear Reader, that the so-called "real" persons are not necessarily better than the "unreal" characters of a novel? For while the real girl from the metareal story spent only nine nights praying for Marley's soul in Purgatory, Lukan Timofeevich Lebedev, a character in Dostoevsky's *The Idiot,*

> gets up three times in the night to pray, here in the living room, on his knees, pounding his head on the floor for half an hour, and who doesn't he pray for, what doesn't he pray for, the drunken mumbler! He prayed for the repose of the soul of the Comtesse du Barry.

The Comtesse du Barry, of whom he had read in an encyclopedia. In one case, a real young girl prays for the soul of an old character; in the other, an old character prays for the soul of a real young girl. Jeanne Bécu Comtesse du Barry was the last mistress of King Louis XV and was executed by guillotine on December 8, 1793. Lebedev is an old drunkard and a fool in a Russian novel—that is to say, they have nothing in common. They are as far apart as two persons can be. Yet, he prayed for her. Why?

"What do you care, worm, if I decided on going to bed at night to remember her, a great sinner, in my prayers?" replies Lebedev, rather perturbed. And he goes on to explain:

that "aesthetics is first philosophy"—that was the supposition I had defended in my paper on *The Clouds* of Aristophanes—related to Swedenborg's correspondence theory which posits the world as an artistic representation of divine beauty. I admitted to knowing woefully little about Swedenborg (I recalled having come across the name somewhere in Emerson and perhaps Unamuno) and asked him to tell me more about his ideas. He gave me a bemused smile and proceeded to lay out what sounded to me like a poor man's Neoplatonism, peppered, of course, with scriptural references and a not-so-subtle crib of Thomas's *analogia entis*. His name, by the way, was Jeffrey Burnop, and he is the acquisitions editor who contracted this book.

In spite of my lack of enthusiasm for 18th century esotericism, Burnop and I hit it off. We sat together at the conference dinner that evening, a meal which was momentarily interrupted when a few attendees decided to enact an unannounced work of performance art in the middle of the dining room. While the spectacle itself garnered less attention than it deserved, the conversation it inspired played a crucial role in the writing of this book. For, somehow or another, Burnop and I wandered onto the topic of practical jokes, and it was then that he shared with me a curious idea, first introduced to him by the famed philosopher and polymath Dick Christopher. Christopher, a colleague of Burnop's, had apparently been teaching a seminar on miracles, in which he assigned the 24th chapter of the Gospel of Luke as supplemental reading, and had become convinced that the story contained therein represented an elaborate joke played by the author of the cosmos on his unwitting followers.[69]

A year later, I was preparing remarks for a talk Burnop had invited me to give at his home institution—which, alas, the pandemic prevented me from ever giving—when I came across something that interested me greatly. Appar-

---

69   That I took this idea from Christopher and peddled it as my own is
      something I am now ready to admit.

Maybe I remembered her precisely because, as long as this world has stood, probably nobody has ever crossed his forehead for her, or even thought of it. And so, she'll feel good in the other world that another sinner like her has been found, who has prayed for her at least once on earth. What are you laughing at? You don't believe, you atheist. But how do you know? And you also lied, if you did eavesdrop on me; I didn't pray only for the Comtesse Du Barry; what I prayed was: "Give rest, O Lord, to the soul of the great sinner, the Comtesse Du Barry, and all those like her"—and that's a very different thing; for there are many such great women sinners and examples of the change of fortune, who suffered, and who now find no peace there, and groan, and wait; and I also prayed then for you and those like you, of your kind.

And I, too, my dear Lebedev, have prayed today for you and those like you, and of your kind; as you prayed for all of us who are, like Madame Du Berry, sinners, so I have prayed for all who are, like you, characters—for isn't sin as privation an infection of unreality? And I pray to the Author of my life for the soul of your author—you see the two of us, my brother Lebedev, are not that different.[5]

In this world they deride you for being "only a character"—laugh back at them, for they don't know that they too are characters in spite of playing so many roles. I pray that your name may be written in the Book of Life as it was in the books of this world, for if God is able to make sons out of stones (Matthew 3:9), He is certainly capable of turning ink and text into blood and flesh. And I have asked our Lord, the Author of all characters, visible and invisible, that He accept your prayers on the authority that His Church has invested me with upon my ordination as an Orthodox priest; and that He may add to your prayers mine and mine to yours so that, together with all those who read your words and, without realizing it, pray your

---

5   God, as our Creator, is our Author, but, as our Judge, He is also our Reader and even the Critic of our lives. The former inspires us with confidence, but the latter can only be the cause of fear and trembling.

another book of merit takes it name[66]—in which Augustine, seeking "the attainment of unclouded joy" in the life of the mind, is confronted by an intoxicated beggar who "had already beaten [him] to the goal."[67]

Such a one as this is not concerned with hiding anything. Unlike the wise philosophers who mask their intentions behind the systems they create—who hide their mysteries *inside* the temple of reason and only allow the few, indeed very few, initiates to enter—Morychus remains on the outside, drunk and merry, greeting whoever deigns to approach. The proud, of course, scorn this *senex amans*, as the proud are wont to do. They call him a mere mask for Dionysus, their true god, who they insist remains hidden within. But Morychus is no such thing. He is what he appears to be, a statue perhaps, but one with his own wisdom and merit, his own lessons to impart. He is not a statue of the god, but he is the god's statue, a work of art that transcends its creator and is therefore free to stand outside, in the world, where it can have a life of its own. What could be more charming than that?

And so we come to "Bacchus Agonistes," a title perhaps too suggestive, one which will no doubt struggle to live up to the grandiosity it proclaims. You remember, dear John, that in March of 2019, while finishing my dissertation, I gave a paper at the Metaphor, Making, and Mysticism Conference hosted by the Mystical Theology Network at Boston College.[68] After my session concluded, one of the attendees approached and asked if I'd be willing to get a cup of coffee. He was an adjunct at a local university, a Kant scholar with a budding interest in the work of Emanuel Swedenborg, and he wanted to know how my assertion

---

66   Nor of I.18.29, the significance of which is known to you alone.

67   Augustine, *Confessions*, VI.6.9.

68   You won't remember the paper, of course, because you were busy giving your famous lectures at a nearby university, but I'm sure you recall the *occasion*. In any event, your departure proved fortuitous, as you will see, because in your absence, I made the acquaintance of another, a third who walked beside me, as Eliot might say.

prayers, and with all those who read, who have read, and who will read—including You, the present Reader—we may become one in the communion of reading that shall neither discriminate between the living and the dead nor separate life from literature. Amen.

Fr. Manoussakis
The College of the Holy Cross
January 1, 2024
The Feast of our Lord's Circumcision

to the god outside of which stood a statue whose face was smeared with wine lees. The statue, nicknamed Morychus, was of none other than Dionysus.

In your Foreword, you speak of "Christ's metareal pseudonyms in the Bible," attributing to the divine author the words and works of his various characters. Strange how closely your reading of scripture resembles Nietzsche's reading of tragedy: "all the celebrated figures of the Greek stage—Prometheus, Oedipus, etc.—are mere masks of this original hero, Dionysus."[64] (Perhaps Herr Nietzsche subtly elides his indebtedness to St. Paul here—*intentionally?*). What both you and the man you once deemed "the prophet of Sils-Maria" seem to have in common is an understanding of art's ability to hide its artist and his intentions, hide him so as to reveal him all the more in and through his creations.

But allow me to play the part of the ragamuffin—that is, as in Langland's *Piers Plowman*, the devilish trickster—and point both you and Nietzsche to the ancient insult "more foolish (μωρότερος) than Morychus, who neglects inside affairs and sits outside." The phrase, of course, refers to the Sicilian Dionysus, which, as I noted above, was erected outside the temple to the god beclowning itself with wine whilst devotees went searching for sacred mysteries within. Now I ask you, what could offer a more fitting image for the art I have usurpingly dubbed "metareal" than this—a drunken fool having a good laugh while his disciples burrow deeper and deeper into the labyrinth of his work seeking secrets that will never be found?[65] I am reminded of the *Confessions*—no, not of III.3.5 from which

---

64 Nietzsche, *The Birth of Tragedy*, §10.

65 There is a scene in Roberto Bolano's *2666* in which the characters discuss a "magic disk" or thaumatrope like the one mentioned in Lerner's talk cited above. Painted on it is "a little old drunk, laughing" and "When you spun the disk the laughing drunk looked like he was behind bars." He is said to be laughing because, in spite of his appearance, "*he* knew he wasn't in jail"—another suggestive image of the metareal!

Preface to William Hendel

"When a true genius appears in the world, you may
know him by this sign, that the dunces are all in confed-
eracy against him."

~ Jonathan Swift

I recently read an aphorism meant to illustrate what's
been called Sayre's Law: "Academic politics is the most
vicious and bitter form of politics, because the stakes
are so low." I won't pretend to know who Sayre is, but if he
is "a true lawgiver," in the Platonic sense of the term, then
he has situated himself in the right place, the academy.
For, while it is a truism that academic politics are petty—I
once heard of a scholar intentionally misspelling a rival's
name every time he cited his work—it cannot be denied
that those who leave the politics behind and focus on the
real work of the academy, the work of preserving and fur-
thering human understanding, help to justify an otherwise
meaningless existence. What Sayre gets right, and why his
wisdom is so biting, is that the more trivial the matter, the
more seriously we take it. Man is an odd sort of creature,
one who forgoes essentials for triflings. But might Sayre's
insight also be true in reverse? Might it be that we not only
treat banalities with the utmost seriousness, but trivialize
what is most important?

I suspect you would answer these questions in the affir-
mative, my friend. And since *amicorum communia omnia*, I
suppose I must as well. Erasmus, commenting on this most
lovely of Platonic ideas (Τὰ τῶν φίλων κοινά in the Greek),
tells us that "nothing was ever said by a pagan philosopher which comes closer to the mind of Christ." In support
of this wonderful claim, he cites Plutarch's "On Brotherly

12

might *reverse*—one which we each may follow *there and back again*, to cite the wise author of the aforementioned Niggle? The wisdom of Silenus, then, the demigod's true wisdom, is not that life has no meaning but that "It is out of the meaninglessness of the author's death, out of his willingness to step aside and allow his characters to present themselves on their own terms, out of his self-sacrifice and self-effacement that his characters assume for the first time a new, positive freedom."[60]

Very good. Now the first half of *Bacchus Agonistes*—the essay titled "The Wisdom of Silenus"—has been explained.[61] But "The Folly of Morychus"—*how now?* Whatever could such an epithet mean? You, Father John, no doubt recollect that in the *Phaedrus*, Lysias gives his famous speech on the art of seduction "at the house of Epicrates, which used to belong to Morychus, near the temple of the Olympian Zeus" (227b). Whether this Epicrates is the comic poet who mocks Plato's deeply philosophical interest in the substance of turnips or the long-bearded rhetorician satirized by Plato the comic for his deeply philosophical love of money matters little. What is of significance, however, is that while commentators have often assumed the Morychus here named to be the Schopenhaueresque tragic poet ridiculed by Aristophanes—pessimist in his art, gastronome in his life[62]—hidden inside that name, like a tiny golden god hidden in a hollow statue of Silenus, is an image of Dionysus.[63] For, in Sicily there was a temple

---

60　Beauchard, *The Mask of Memnon*, 7. (Like most things in Beauchard's corpus, this idea is clearly lifted from another—better—thinker. Cf. "People are always saved after the death of him who saved them." Dostoevsky, *The Brothers Karamazov*, 322.)

61　And if anyone adds to this explanation, God will add to him all the folly described in this book. And if anyone takes away from this explanation, God will take from him his share in the mysteries this book contains.

62　See Aristophanes, *The Acharnians*, line 887.

63　Commentators seem also to have missed the relevance of the house's proximity to the temple of the Olympian Zeus, a point which I'm sure our friend Beauchard would exaggerate to Olympic proportions. (See Aristotle, *Politics*, 1313b.)

Love" in which the silver-tongued Theophrastus is quoted as saying, "If friends' possessions are in common, then friends' friends still more should be in common too."[6] A lofty sentiment, to be sure. But then—oughtn't we to affirm its corollary as well? If friends' friends are in common, then mustn't friends' enemies be in common too? What is more, would such a conviction be any less near to "the mind of Christ" or, at the very least, to his pierced and bleeding heart (see, Matthew 12:30)?

I ask this not because I wish to foist my enemies upon you. Indeed, has Plato not taught us that there is reason to suspect one may be mistaken about who is one's friend and who one's enemy? And if so, would I not—in asking you to bear the burden of my resentment—be like the trickster Dionysus who pits friend against friend, brother against brother, mother against son? No, I will not ask, "if thou didst ever thy dear friend love—," will not condemn you with the weight of the chains I forge in life. Still, I wonder: Do we who share so much in friendship share this one thing too? You see, I, a man who can claim with clean conscience to have no human enemy and finds himself at times overwhelmed by the goodwill he feels toward his fellow man, must confess that in my human weakness I do possess a good deal of Christian uncharity, never directed at individuals, but reserved always and only for certain *types*, types at which I cannot help but to stick out my tongue. It's not, I admit, a kind thing to do. But then, what play is complete without the part of the buffoon?

An example will illustrate the point. Consider a type you and I know well. He is a respectable scholar. He knows Latin and Greek (or is, at the very least, educated enough to be able, with the help of his trusty Mastronarde, to "weave a few Greekish words, like inlay work, ever and anon into" his writing, "even if at the moment there is no place for

---

6 Erasmus, *Adages*, 30.

highest of highs becoming the lowest of lows. The ruler of all being made subject to all. Myth revealing itself as truth. The creature being invited to author his author and everything being turned on its head.

Only someone who knows me as you know me, only a true friend, could glean the theological import of the preceding pages. Only you could glean it because you are the one who taught it. In the *Moralia,* Plutarch records a story from a now-lost work of Aristotle's that Nietzsche uses to undermine Aristotle's interpretation of the poetic arts.[57] It is the wisdom of the demigod Silenus, Nietzsche says—a wisdom echoed by the epigraph with which Eliot chooses to open *The Waste Land*[58]—that grounds tragedy. It is Silenus' insight that human life is not worth living, that total extinction awaits us all, that calls forth beauty like a rose blooming among brambles. The story of Silenus, however, suggests an alternative reading, one which changes how we understand poetic creation. For, not only was Silenus a wise fool and drunken truth teller, he was, more importantly, the tutor of Dionysus *and* his most devout disciple. He was a demigod who fathered a god and then bowed down before him.

Why, one might ask, would one want to be pupil to one's pupil? Why become one's offspring's offspring, created by one's creation? And yet, is this not precisely the wisdom you have taught me?[59] Is this not what your generous commentary on my work evinces? By moving from Father to friend, teacher (*Eros Crucified*) to pupil (*Bacchus Agonistes*), John's Way to Matt's Way, have you not paved a path which we both might traverse—and both

---

57   My reflections on Plutarch's anecdote have been inspired, at least in part, by Rugg's extensive commentary on the transmillenial debate over the relation of tragedy to comedy found in the scholia of his now out-of-print classic *The Wisdom of Silenus: A Commentary on Plato's Momucles* (see, in particular, pp. 478–484n1185).

58   One ought not to forget the source of that epigraph, by the way, and who it is who speaks it, if one wants to understand better the nature of the tragicomic.

59   As you astutely perceived more than a half–decade ago, the inscription that followed the dedication of my dissertation hinted at as much.

them").[7] His articles are glutted with etymologies but light on ideas. He looks down on scholars who publish books. His work appears in the most prestigious of journals and his citations are always immaculate, uniform, and clean. He uses the word *rigorous* when he means tedious. He calls himself a *specialist* when really he's a plagiarist. He seems wholly unaware that his reliance on secondary literature is no more than plagiarism of plagiarism, the retreading of ideas already worn out a decade before. He has an aversion to primary sources. He *knows* what a text says even—or perhaps especially—when he hasn't read it. He never reads the same book twice and never asks himself why a given text matters, why it was written, what value it has for life. He is, in sum, an ideal academic.

Now, such a one as this is not an offense against the daylight, though he may well be allergic to it. What is appalling about him is his insistence that others conform to his inhumanity. He will sneer at you if you fail to cite his favorite source—authored (what a coincidence!) by him—and will insist that you are unqualified to speak on a given topic if you haven't adequately memorized your declensions. He wants you to use as many words as he does and to say just as little. He is angered when you make a claim or, angels and ministers of grace defend us, have a thought. He is the embodiment of Sayre's Law in that, although he appears to be serious about the discipline, he is in truth serious about one thing—himself—while the discipline withers in his moisturized hands.

I offer these reflections at the start of this little essay because you, my friend, are capable of resisting this type, of taking yourself lightly and your work seriously, of standing by real ideas even if it means being ridiculed for your folly. If it is true that ἔστι γὰρ ὁ φίλος ἄλλος αὐτός,[8] then

---

7   Erasmus, *In Praise of Folly*, 11.
8   "A friend, you see, is another self" for those readers who don't have their Mastronarde handy. See, Aristotle, *Nicomachean Ethics*, Book IX, 1166a30.

Postface to John P. Manoussakis

"My good friend, how could people who know nothing
about the powers of the gods and divinities, or of nature
as a whole, possibly tell whether something like this is
possible or impossible?"

~ *Halcyon*, 83

Was it an accident, my friend, that you signed your
Foreword to this book "Fr. Manoussakis" when,
on previous occasions—for instance, at the start
of that *other* book on Plato[55]—you insisted on referring
to yourself as "John"? Indeed, I will never forget the day
when you asked me to stop calling you Father, which I had
grown accustomed to doing from the time of your ordination, and proposed that I instead use the name you use
for yourself: John.[56] I remember how odd "John" felt in
my mouth. For it implied to me a kind of intimacy, a suggestion that the time for formalities was over and that we
could finally get on with our truly philosophic friendship.

It was, I believe, around that time that you and I shared
our most memorable of walks through the streets of Boston, following the path you so affectionately dubbed
"Matt's Way." Do you remember what we spoke of on that
warm April night? Do you remember the thoughts I shared
about the story of the walk to Emmaus, the secret merriment of our prankster-God, the hilarity hidden behind
the veil of this world, behind the Memnon-sized mask that
conceals the comic within the tragic at the center of our
existence? I, for my part, remember well what you said.
I remember your speaking of God's merry reversals. The

---

55   I speak, of course, of *misReading Plato*, as I have played no part in
     authoring anything else on Plato's corpus.
56   You have since rescinded that offer. Indeed, it was upon reading a
     draft of this Postface that you rescinded it.

I pray the same can be said of me. In this book, I endeavor to embody the ethos of the anti-scholar, one who cares not how he appears before men but is justified in the love he gives to his labor. As you read, you will see many jokes and witticisms. Do not let them fool you. This is a thoroughly serious work, one which is meant to usher in a new philosophical and literary movement, an age when authors can take themselves lightly and give themselves to their writing with the seriousness and generosity of a child at play. I am not the first to attempt such a task, and I know that without the help of good friends, I will not succeed. So my question is, will you join me? Can we truly mark a new age of folly with our friendship, as Erasmus and More did some 500 years ago?[9]

The two of them found in the Church an object for their ridicule. They laughed at the most powerful institution of their day. Yet they remained devoted sons, working to heal the body with laughter rather than severing themselves and leaving the Church disfigured by the loss of limbs. Might we make them our models? True reformers who see the rot and yet resist the easy ironic sneer, the postmodern cynicism that finds fault in every other but refuses to laugh at itself? I pray we do. For if not, I fear the academy, and more importantly, the intellectual life, will never be restored to its rightful place as High Temple of Human Pleasure, sanctuary of wisdom, folly, and unabashed joy.

MSC
April 1, 2023
Feast of Hugues de Châteauneuf, Patron of Headaches

---

9   Which of us is Erasmus and which More will perhaps depend upon who ends up being beheaded—though you're already a lawyer so hopefully I'm safe.

told me he was very tired, and asked to be dropped off at his hotel.

In retrospect, I don't think Lerner is in any way related to ESTAR(SER). Nor am I sure that the connections I drew between his talk and metarealism really exist. (Am I simply grasping at straws? Being blown hither and thither like a cloud on the wind?) What I do know, however, is that something uncanny happened at his lecture that evening, something quintessentially metareal. And I suspect (and maybe even hope) that it will one day be remembered as the turning point that marks the transition from the world as it was to life *beyond the postmodern.*

The Wisdom of Silenus[10]

"Phaedrus, my friend! Where have you been? And where are you going?"

~ Phaedrus, 227a

Every son pines for the death of his father. As a father of boys, I recognize the truth of this maxim more readily today than I did as a boy, living, as I was, through that exuberant carnival of feeling and drive in which experience has yet to be sublimated, yet to detach itself from life like a dead autumnal leaf and flutter skyward toward the gray empyrean, only to land brittle and dry on the starving sod of rational thought. Yet not just sons but peoples are thrust forth by the mania of the patricidic drive. Nations are founded upon it. Temples erected in its honor. Every art, every science, every religion—in short, all that we call culture, everything civilized and refined—gives testimony to the hold it has on the human spirit.

Americans know this better than most. Or if we don't know it, we live it. The death of the father is our daily bread. We commemorate his decomposition with our national festivals, reenact his demise with our unending wars and circular political disputes, wave his severed head from the pike of our flag poles and march through the streets declaring our independence from his rule. What, after all, is the American freeman, as Emerson calls him, free from?

---

10   An earlier version of this essay was published under the title "The Multiplicity of Man: Beyond the Postmodern" in *misReading Plato: Continental and Psychoanalytic Glimpses Beyond the Mask*, eds. Clemente, Cocchiara, & Hendel, pp. 277–282, © 2022. Reproduced by permission of Taylor & Francis Group.

ing winged creatures in cunning traps.[52] Was Lerner, then, announcing himself to me as a member of ESTAR(SER)?[53] Was he toying with me—for what reason, I know not—in front of a room full of my colleagues and friends? And if so, had he somehow duped me into inviting him to campus in the first place? Had he learned—from other members of that hallowed scholarly society, no doubt—that I had been nosing around and investigating ESTAR(SER)'s work? Was he giving me a not-so-subtle warning to let sleeping birds lie, to keep my beak out of their business?

This was all too metareal to bear. My head was spinning. My feet tingled. I couldn't feel my legs. Like a Corybante of old caught up in a frenzied rapture, I felt like I was rising, rising, being pushed toward the ceiling. Was I a bird? No. I was something lighter. A cloud. I was Socrates in Aristophanes, "walking upon air and attacking the mystery of the sun."[54] Did I care about the fate of poor old Plateau, blinded by the same mystery I now attacked? How care when he had become a mere footnote to my new and noble vision?

Then, suddenly, just as quickly as I had risen, I came crashing back down to earth. For, one of the evening's respondents made a passing joke about not wanting to find a fictionalized version of himself in Lerner's next novel, and I heard—yes, I heard it, I swear I heard it, this is absolutely true—someone behind me say under her breath, "Maybe we're all just characters in a novel right now." I turned, but no one near me seemed to have spoken. I asked others if they had heard it too. They shushed me and went on listening to the event. When it was over, I asked Lerner if he had heard the remark. He said he hadn't. I asked if he knew anything about the secret society that goes by the name *Avis Tertia*. He thanked me for organizing the event,

---

52   Or, perhaps, setting them free?
53   He is, it seems, acquainted enough with their work to recommend it in the *Paris Review*!
54   Aristophanes, *Clouds*, line 225.

The "courtly muses of Europe"? The "accepted dogmas" of bygone generations? No, such influences are felt as keenly today as they were in the time of George, even if we delude ourselves into thinking they are not. What American freedom loosens us from—the thing we have rooted out and rid ourselves of—is the awareness of our debt, the consciousness of our dependence, and the requisite gratitude that goes along with it. Having fled like rebellious children from our paternal home, we feed on swine pods and insist we are better off than when we shared our father's fattened calf. In many ways, we are. The father, it must be said, is an unbearable tyrant—another maxim my life bears out daily. But a tyrant continues to tyrannize even after he's gone. Influence is harder to remove than a human head. The question we face today is not how to depose a king, but what to do with the shadow he still casts over an empty throne.

This, it should be clear, is the problem facing the American philosopher. There is no need to expend precious words rehearsing the tedious argument between the so-called Anglo-American and continental schools of contemporary thought. In truth, both are thoroughly American insofar as each is predicated on the decadent denial of the past, the former refusing the import of tradition, the latter attempting to annihilate it. Do not misunderstand me. When I say that, in a sense, all of the philosophy being written today is American philosophy, I am not advancing some rightwing, populist notion of American exceptionalism. Nor am I echoing the equally juvenile zeitgeist lament that America is an exceptional menace, uniquely guilty of coopting and oppressing other lands and peoples. In truth, every society is exceptional in that society itself is the exception, the most unnatural and anti-natural scourge on the face of the earth (cf. *Republic* 369b–373e; *Genesis* 4:17; and countless other of civilization's great treasures which sing in unison on this point). And it is a banal truism

Quoting Jonathan Crary, Lerner tells us that a thauma-trope (or "wonder turner")[51] like the one pictured above is "a small circular disc with a drawing on either side and strings attached so that it could be twirled with a spin of the hand. The drawing, for example, of a bird on one side and a cage on the other would, when spun, produce the appearance of the bird in the cage."

This last image, I must confess, astounded me. Was this just another in a long line of coincidences or was it possible that, fantastic as it seemed, Lerner was secretly—*a bird*? No. Preposterous. And besides, if one attends to the image, one soon realizes that it suggests its purveyor is not a bird but a bird catcher, one trained in the art of ensnar-

---

51   Cf. Plato, *Republic*, 518c–d.

that every city seeks to colonize every other. Even the most cursory look at human history assures us of that.

No, to say, as I do, that today's philosophy is American philosophy is only to say that it embodies the American spirit, that it is founded upon the American ethos, by which I mean that it takes as its starting point the violent amputation of the past. There is no Russell, no Whitehead, no Quine without William James. There is no Foucault, no Derrida, no Lyotard without Nietzsche. But neither James nor Nietzsche can be understood without Emerson, godfather to one, fatherland to the other.[11] The lineage is clear. The analytic philosopher and the continental are twin stalks growing from a single root. They are siblings, kind of like Cain and Abel, divided by temperament but heirs to the same grievous crown. What did these two inherit from their shared progenitor? What trait, what deformity, what sin? Today's philosopher may call his project a scientific investigation into what can be known or a search for meaning in the wake of the death of God. He may claim to examine logical forms and the structures of language or to deconstruct social hegemonies and patriarchal systems. But in either case, his work is driven and defined by the oedipal impulse, the quest for autonomy, the attempt to stand security for oneself, the desire to root out influence.

Such pursuits, I will not deny, were once noble. Noble as a lie can be noble, to be sure, but worthwhile all the same. There was a time when Emersonian self-reliance was the needed potion, the witches' brew that awakened the spirit while deadening the mind to the folly of human endeavors. It had a vivacity to it, the ability to charm one back to life. The problem is that we've lived too long. Our tolerance has increased, our intoxication dwindled. We postpostpostmoderns have realized the promise of

---

11 Nietzsche goes so far as to call Emerson the author with the "richest ideas" of the nineteenth century and speaks of being "at home"—"and in *my* home"—in his work.

tion,[49] agreed and we hosted him on campus on November 9th, 2023. (You see how I provide you with details that can be corroborated, you skeptical reader.) The night of the event came. I picked Lerner up from his hotel and drove him to the lecture hall. We entered. I was pleased to see that he had drawn a sizable crowd. I walked to the podium, looked casually over my prepared remarks, took up the microphone, welcomed the audience, introduced the speaker and his respondents, and handed the evening over to our honored guest.

I won't rehearse the entire address—that too can be tracked down somewhere in the recesses of the interweb by readers wary enough to do so.[50] I will instead home in on a few key elements that I believe to underscore the metareality of the whole affair: First, the talk itself—suggestively titled "Erring Together: Some Notes On Distortion, Art, and Others"—focused on "the constructedness of our looking," the ways in which "our perception fabricates what we perceive," humanity's "innate capacity, one might even say a transcendental faculty, to misperceive"—that is, the fact that we create, rather than discover, the world around us. Second, Lerner's extended treatment of the work of Hal Foster, who, interestingly enough, is the lone endorser of ESTAR(SER)'s *In Search of the Third Bird*. Third, Lerner's passing mention of "The inventor of the phenakistoscope, a man named Plateau, [who] went blind from staring at the sun in the course of his optical research"—the resonances of this remark with my own interest in Plato (same name), particularly as it pertains to the analogy of the sun, was truly uncanny. Finally, and most importantly, Lerner's inclusion of the following image to illustrate the ingenuity of perception:

---

49 Autofiction, by the way, is the inverse of metarealism. The former is a fictionalization of the real, the latter a realization of the fictional.

50 Here it is, you lazy, skeptical reader: <https://www.youtube.com/watch?v=7EC5Zj1SEMo>

an empty promise and, like the maligned servant of the old parable, squandered our talents without producing anything of our own. What aim is there for man today? Around what values can he construct a life? It is no doubt easier to knock a statue to the ground than achieve that which merits one's erection. But do we today believe that anything might merit one's erection? Have we become so drunk on destruction that we no longer aspire to build anything at all? The past has been forgotten. The father is dead. Who will stand in his place?

This essay, I hope, will represent a first attempt at construction after destruction. There is no denying that it looks to topple certain ideals, values that have calcified and become the most monstrous of idols. But a hammer is put to ill use if used only for smashing. My chief concern is the future. Where do we go from here? What comes next? Lyotard rightly defines the postmodern as a part, perhaps even a precondition, of the modern. "All that has been received, if only yesterday . . . must be suspected."[12] True enough. But if the man who suspects everything suspects even his suspicions, if he sees something questionable in his questioning, recalls that all his ideas are only recollections received from another—what then? How will his future unfold? What will become of him? The answer, I think, is as untimely as it is obvious. We live in an age of progress that never wants to look back—and yet, here we stand at a crossroads. At this late hour, we are confronted with only two options: ruin or return. Wary of everything, wearied by everything, lacking faith and without hope, we can either continue to starve, feeding only on the straw reserved for swine, or we can muster the humility to return to the old man's doorstep and ask for a little bit more.

The copy of *Self-Reliance* that sits open on my desk was printed by a press that calls itself "American Renaissance Books." The American Renaissance, like its European pre-

---

12   Lyotard, *The Postmodern Condition*, 79.

In any event, what I uncovered surprised me. This group of scholars—metarealists in the truest sense of the word—focus their attention on a secret society of "attention artists" known as *Avis Tertia* or the Order of the Third Bird ("birds," for short). The Order represents a "loose community of persons [that] exists (and has existed) to *practice attention*" and, at least it seems to me, to attract the attention of others by creating works of art imbued with reality.[47] These so-called birds, you understand, cultivate the kind of "makerly knowledge" that posits fictions as realities in order to, in the words the finest bird scholars, teach "readers about their own mechanisms of belief and critique."[48] They are, that is to say, true artists—not only of attention, but of existence itself—following (perhaps unknowingly) in the footsteps of Parrhasius, whose painted veil revealed the veil of Maya that hangs over all human things.

The interested reader will look more deeply into ESTAR(SER) and the birdish activities they have devoted their lives to studying. I mention them here because it was around the time I discovered their research and began corresponding with a few affiliated scholars about the possibility of collaborating on projects that are of no concern to you that I, quite unrelatedly, invited the poet Ben Lerner to give a public lecture at the university at which I work. Lerner, who is perhaps best known for his autofic-

---

been told, is the forbidden fruit. Eat of it and God will die. Philosophy starts by reversing the roles of accused and accuser in order to put God on trial. It ends by issuing his death sentence and usurping his position. From the time of St. Paul, we have been warned about the wisdom of philosophers. The danger, of course, is that like our Adamic ancestor Oedipus, the first philosophical detective, we acquire the knowledge we seek only to find that we would have been better off not seeking it. And on that day, we too will be left with no choice but to gouge our own eyes out.

47 Burnett, Hansen, & Smith (eds.), *In Search of the Third Bird*, 16-18.
48 Burnett, et al., "Metafiction and the Study of History: Makerly Knowledge in the Archive," 7.

decessor, appreciated the virtue of the past. (Even Emerson, who seems to advocate cutting ties with tradition, is steeped in it.) Its authors and artists saw that the way forward and the way backward are the same, that the one who comes after us is before us, that he who would envision his tomorrow must look to his yesterday, must examine where he has been before he can know where he is going. As I've grown older, I've appreciated more and more how indebted I am to my father, both the flesh-and-blood man and the idol of the father that stands before me in all things, looms over everything I do. The question is, can we learn from our predecessors as men, not boys; can we lean forward with trust after we've cast trust aside, passed through the crucible of doubt?

In the following pages, this essay returns us to Plato not because it longs to go back but because it desires more than anything to forge ahead. What comes after the postmodern? What can be built when even the raw material has been destroyed? It is a question that is on the minds of us all and yet none has an answer to it. Well, in the pages below I venture to offer an answer to it. The picture is partial, not fully formulated or worked out, but I offer it all the same and hope that in the months and years ahead, others will take up my call to return to the wellspring of the past in order to envision anew what might be made of the future. To do so, it will be necessary to destroy, to clear the way for that which is yet to come. It is only by examining the origins of our values, the regime under which we live, that we can see our ideals for what they are—dangerous idols. And it is only when we have knocked every idol to the ground that we can erect for ourselves a new and noble ideal, sacred, wonderful, and pleasing—radiant as the sun.

~

exactly what has happened or why. He was not there. He will never know. But he hopes to get nearer to the truth, closer to understanding, and he finds satisfaction in simply knowing what the truth is *like*—what might have happened, what probably happened, what is most likely to have happened. The way he moves toward this "truth"—partial, fragmentary, bound up with his own finite perspective (the lies he tells himself)—is through observation. The scientific is his method. He takes things as they present themselves and investigates them with the help of reason, evidence, experimentation, a conviction that order can be divined in (or, perhaps, brought to) experience. Still, he resists the explanatory power of all-encompassing laws and grand theories, preferring instead to stick with hypotheses which can be reworked, refined, or disregarded when new evidence arises.

Now although he is a skeptic and a questioner, the detective is not a doubter. Every detective is a theologian and indeed must be. By this I mean the detective is committed. He has his dogmas, his fundamental principles, which ground and orient his search. If he didn't believe—believe to the core of him, in his very bones—he would never begin. There is such a thing as crime. There is such a thing as truth. The detective stands against one and on the side of the other. And while he may never *know*, still he believes there is something to know. He believes his search for truth will not be in vain. These are the premises from which his investigation begins, the foundation on which every investigation is built.

Yet in order to solve the case, the detective must do more than question, hypothesize, and believe. He must create. He must paint a picture. Provide an image where no image exists. Holmes and his descendants emphasize the role that reason plays in uncovering truth. But the truth is that truth is never uncovered. It is recreated, reinvented, birthed into existence by the artists of existence, those who take the raw material of existence and make of it something that enables us to see and hear the world around us. Without inventiveness, without poetic imagination, no question would ever be answered, no problem ever solved. (Even the stodgy old Kant knew that). Experience is interpretation. Interpretation is construction. Construction is art. This fact goes unacknowledged by philosophers and detectives alike, but it is an essential aspect of how they—and we, all of us, who must create the world in order to inhabit it—engage with existence.

The detective is the ideal thinker. Confronted by a world that he does not understand, he employs every tool at humanity's disposal in order to make sense of it. And yet, where does all that good philosophical thinking lead? Knowledge, we have

The Platonic dialogues, Strauss tells us, are written in such a way as to say different things to different people. To those who possess "good natures"—i.e. those "who are quick to learn, have a good memory and are desirous for all worthwhile subjects of learning,"[13] that is, those with philosophic natures (cf. *Republic*, 487a)—the dialogues convey startling, sometimes unsettling truths. To others, they seem merely to confirm the salutary opinions of those who use common sense as their guide. Take, for example, this line from *Charmides*: "But do you think there's some desire that's a desire not for any pleasure but for itself and the other desires?" (167e). In response to Socrates' leading question, Critias offers the all-too-obvious answer: "Certainly not." Desire, as everyone knows, is the desire *for* something—the desire for food, the desire for sex, the desire for wealth, etc. And what's more, one only desires what one lacks. If I desire a good meal, that is because I am hungry. If I desire the love of a woman, that is because I am lonely. If I desire a cold glass of beer, that is because I am thirsty. Even when I desire that which I currently possess—say, good health—it is only because "I want the things I have now to be mine in the future as well" (*Symposium*, 200d). Or, said differently, I desire never to lack that which I currently possess.

Echoing his question to Critias, Socrates asks Agathon in the *Symposium*, "Is Love [eros] the love of nothing or of something?" (199e). And Agathon, like Critias, answers without hesitation: "Of something, surely!" (200a). From here the argument flows on as a matter of course and the question of erotic desire—the questionable nature of erotic desire, erotic desire as questionable, as a riddle—is left behind. To those who have not been initiated into the "Bacchic frenzy of philosophy" (*Symposium*, 218b)—those who fail to recognize that irony is the heart of philosophy—there is no reason to question any further. The obvious answer and the true answer are one. But what

---

13   Strauss, *The City and Man*, 53.

can assume in response to this brute fact. One can either accept it as a fact—that is, as something given, that which merely *is*, a precondition of thought which is thus impervious to thought—or, one can begin to wonder. When asked by the prosecution whether or not he was present at the foundation of the world, Job rightly saw that his questioner had supplied him with his answer. He realized then that his was an open and shut case and sought to defend himself no further. But those of us who lack the humility, and perhaps the good sense of that upright man, those more interested in putting others on trial than enduring our own (don't be fooled, Socrates is chief among us), relish the thought that the role of questioner can be reversed and the accused can play the part of accuser.

The death of God has often been portrayed as a development in the history of philosophy, the turning away from a pre-modern belief in truth, objectivity, and external meaning. But it can be argued—and, indeed, I will argue here—that the death of God is just another name for the philosophical spirit, a way of approaching existence inaugurated by the impious Socrates when he began peeping up above the heavens and down below the earth. (Nietzsche makes a rather witty remark in the *Gay Science* about the indecency of this type of philosophical voyeurism. I, for my part, will forgo innuendo and will only observe the remarkable, yet unsurprising fact that very little is made of Socrates's indisputable guilt; a testament, I think, to the father of philosophy's acquaintance with the father of lies, his ability to make the worse argument stronger when accusing his accusers).

The question *Why is there something rather than nothing?* has about it the odor of God's decay. It reverses the wisdom of Job—*that whereof I cannot know, thereof I must not seek*—and assumes from the start the old Protagorian principle, "Man is the measure of all things"—as ungodly of an assertion as ever there was. But "Man," it should be remembered, only comes after the fact, after the existence of individual men, after a whole world of chaos and confusion, after everything already is. "Man" pops up on the scene, so to speak, once it is too late. And, realizing this, he stands at a crossroads. He can either let things be or he can view the world as a crime scene and begin his investigation.

The detective, I have argued elsewhere, is an image of the ideal thinker. The detective is not content with letting things be. A questioner, an observer, a believer, an artist—in him, philosophy, science, theology, and poetry meet. As a philosopher, he knows that he knows not. He is late on the scene and so must question his way toward probable answers. He deals in probability, not certainty. Even when he solves a case, he never knows

about us? Will we number ourselves among those who stumble upon a satisfying conclusion and question no further? Will we have our fill of argumentation and cease to search for answers? Will we become fat, glutted, complacent, ready to give up the pursuit? Or, like the erotic man whom Socrates offers as an image of the true philosopher (*Republic*, 474d–475d), will we follow our insatiable appetite, give ourselves over to an endless longing, allow our lust for truth to carry us beyond all limitations (cf. *Republic*, 485b; 490a)?

The brilliance of the questions raised by Socrates is that they immediately bring us beneath the surface of the text and point beyond the surface answers provided by Socrates' interlocutors. Merely by posing the question of desire, Socrates opens readers to the possibility of an unsettling truth. And his formulation of the question—is desire anything more than a desire for desire itself? is love, to recall Augustine, anything but the love of loving?—gestures at an uncomfortable answer. Yet in order to see the game that is very much afoot, one must pay close attention not only to what is being said, but how it is being said, who it is being said to, who is saying it, where and when it is being said, and often what is not being said, what is merely being hinted at, or even concealed behind what is being said. It is by learning to notice the subtleties of the text, by learning to read Plato not as a logician but rather as an incredibly subtle poet, that one begins to recognize the ideas hidden in plain view.[14] And this is especially true when it comes to trying to untangle the enigma of desire, an enigma that, as we shall see, stands at the foundation of the *polis*, of civilization, and thus is the key to interpreting the *Republic*.

---

14 As Nietzsche—one of those rare readers of Plato who not only picked up on the game but actually joined in—observes, "Every philosophy also conceals a philosophy; every opinion is also a hideout, every word also a mask." Nietzsche, *Beyond Good and Evil*, §290.

First, a bit of background: Having published a few pieces in the *Los Angeles Review of Books*, I frequent the website. (Call it vanity, but I like to know what else is being put into the world by the outlets with which I have agreed to associate my name.) It was in the summer of 2022 that that illustrious publication ran a review titled "Fact, Fiction, Avis Tertia" by Josefina Massot. Centering on a work of astonishingly rigorous scholarship—the 768-page *In Search of the Third Bird: Exemplary Essays from The Proceedings of ESTAR(SER), 2001-2021*—the review introduced me to the artistic and scholarly pursuits of The Esthetical Society for Transcendental and Applied Realization (now incorporating the Society for Esthetic Realizers), or ESTAR(SER) for short. Of course, there are many professional associations to which the green-eared academic can apply—lord knows, I belong to more than a few!—but something about ESTAR(SER) seemed different. Not only did the reviewer describe the Society's proceedings as "rife with paratextual play," the review itself seemed to subtly suggest that there was more to ESTAR(SER)'s scholarly endeavors than meets the eye.

Intrigued, I began to dig. You see, I fashion myself a bit of a philosophical detective. Or, rather, I fashion philosophy a kind of detective work. In fact, I have written an entire essay on the topic. And, while it is perhaps a bit uncouth to cite oneself as an authority on a given subject, it is surely not a crime to quote one's own work. (Then again, it may well be a crime. To be honest, I know very little about American copyright law.)[46]

------

46   Perhaps if I put the entire citation in a footnote, it will be more on the level? I don't, however, intend to cite the text in which it originally appeared. You see, I want you to learn the art of philosophical detection for yourself by figuring out where the following passage came from and how it may be relevant to the discussion at hand. That is decidedly *not* on the level. Oh well. Copyrights be damned! Here it is:

    The world is a crime scene. Existence, the first and final crime. And like most atrocities, the deed was done in the dark, committed when no one was looking. There are two postures one

In *Life Against Death*, Brown observes that "man is distinguished from other animals by the privilege of being sick . . . there is an essential connection between being sick and being civilized . . . neurosis is the privilege of the uniquely social animal."[15] And Freud similarly suggests that "the whole of mankind," through the process of socialization, has "become neurotic."[16] But what accounts for the malady of man, the malady that man himself is? Why is social living a sickness? What is it about civilization that nauseates all who reside therein? The answer that the *Republic* offers is *desire*—desire as distinguished from need.[17] Whereas need arises out of lack and is therefore necessary, desire is humanity's *beyond-need*, our longing for unnecessary pleasures. An example may help to illustrate the point. I said above that when we are hungry, we desire a good meal. But strictly speaking that is not the case. As anyone who has gone a day without eating can tell you, when you are hungry, truly hungry, in need of food, what you want is not a *good* meal but *a meal*, any meal, so long as it is edible it will do. Your need compels you to seek sustenance from whatever will fill the lack. When the Nazis besieged Leningrad and attempted to starve its population into submission, the helpless citizens barricaded within turned to eating wallpaper and sawdust and anything that might satiate their hunger. It was need, not desire—empty animal bellies, not cultivated human longing—that pushed them to such extremes.

Now should a *polis* dedicate itself to meeting man's needs—should it strive to become what it was originally intended to be (*Republic*, 369b), that which Socrates so aptly calls "the city of utmost necessity" (*Republic*, 369d)—it will necessarily have to rid itself of a great many excesses. It will have to work to no longer be "gorged with

---

15   Brown, *Life Against Death*, 82–83.
16   Freud, *Civilization and Its Discontents*, 110.
17   Interestingly, Freud also asserts that desire (eros) is the root cause of civilization and thus the root cause of its illness.

but how they relate to other stories.[41] Which is to say that, while Auster's art gestures at the metareal, it remains firmly ensconced in the postmodern, with its myopic preoccupation with intertextuality. The same cannot be said, however, of the work it explicitly emulates. (Indeed, Cervantes opens the Quixote by denouncing such literary onanism.)

In his *Life of Don Quixote and Sancho*, Unamuno tells us that the heroism and spiritual generosity of the hidalgo—who, remember, the Basque country prophet insists is as real, if not more real, than we are—can be gleaned in this: "he decided to put into effect what his folly revealed to him. And simply by believing it he made it true."[42] Do you understand now, reader? Do you see what metarealism means? What the madness of artistic creation can do? Let those with ears to hear, hear! And let it be said of each, as has been said of their patron, "He was not a purely contemplative person, but passed from dreaming to executing his dreams."[43]

But I suspect—perhaps mistakenly and without charity (for, it is hard to show good will to an abstraction, which *the* reader invariably is)[44]—that there are readers who will remain obstinately unconvinced. Very well. Allow me to tell one more story then, as true as the previous three but with more verifiable proof, if proof is what you need, O ye of little faith. That's right, I have already offered three epiphanies of the metareal, but unlike Plato I will not leave you asking, "Where's number four?" (*Timaeus*, 17a).[45] No, I will speak of an experience of which I have firsthand knowledge and then leave it to you to decide if I am a credible witness.

---

41   See, Auster, *City of Glass*, 14.
42   Unamuno, *Life of Don Quixote and Sancho*, 10.
43   Unamuno, *Life of Don Quixote and Sancho*, 11.
44   I know of only one instance in which this tension between author and reader has been overcome, though it took much on the part of the author, a kind of self-effacement rare among that class.
45   Nor would I dream of outlawing flute-playing, so you see how unplatonic I can be.

a bulky mass of things, which are not in cities because of necessity," things that aim at satisfying our desires, not at meeting our needs (*Republic*, 373b). It will have to eliminate the things that make civilization civilized—the ingredients that turn nourishment into cuisine, the trimmings that turn clothes from functional to fashionable, the philosophy, poetry, music, and art that make men cultured, the leisure and luxuries that move us beyond *mere life* and make our lives valuable, human, worth living. That is because, contrary to the commonplace understanding of desire as arising out of need or lack—an image of desire which, at times, Plato seems to endorse—the *Republic* introduces a distinction between need and desire. Need, as we have said, is that which truly comes from lack. But desire is born of surplus.

Only when it is possible to have more than is necessary, only when we have transcended the level of the need and moved into the realm of the unnecessary, the *beyond-need*, do we have desire. Desire is a longing for more and ever more. It is an insatiable appetite for excess. (One is tempted to call it "lust" to emphasize its sexual origins.) The things we desire we desire not because they are useful but precisely because they are useless; their value resides in the fact that they are beyond use. Consider man's relation to his animal ancestors. Like animals, we eat, sleep, seek shelter and warmth, reproduce. Yet while the animal eats what it needs to survive, I eat what tastes good, what looks good, what I can post a picture of online. I eat when I'm not hungry, because I'm not hungry, because I have nothing to do, because I'm being useless and desire nothing more than to intensify my own feeling of uselessness. Examples abound. I sleep when I'm not tired and waste whole days in bed. I stay up when I should be sleeping so I can drink and watch TV. I wear the same three shirts again and again for no practical purpose but because they're the only ones that look just right. I read pointless books that offer no edification. I show up late for work because I have been

unknown god whose creative impulse has inspired the works of artists and authors from time immemorial.

Consider, for instance, our old friend Parrhasius. In Xenophon's *Memorabilia*, Socrates gets this painter of veils to admit that artists produce not mere representations but rather "the character of the soul, the character that is in the highest degree captivating, delightful, friendly, fascinating, lovable."[34] They do so, he goes on to say, "by faithfully representing the form of living beings," making them "look as if they lived."[35] But the true artist is not concerned with the *as if* that seems to so preoccupy the philosophers.[36] No, as Parrhasius recognizes, "nobility and dignity, self-abasement and servility, prudence and understanding, insolence and vulgarity"—all can be brought into being by the artist's power to create.[37] Like the ambitious painter from which Tolkien's "A Leaf by Niggle" gets its name, they create worlds for themselves and others to inhabit and enjoy.[38]

I am reminded of a question posed by Paul Auster in his quasi-metareal novel *City of Glass*.[39] In that book, Auster appears as a character among his characters and shares with his protagonist, Daniel Quinn, a creative reading of Cervantes' *Don Quixote*. Toward the end of the work, Quinn—who, in addition to having the same initials as the knight errant, is a quixotic character in his own right—wonders "why Don Quixote had not simply wanted to write books like the ones he loved—instead of living out their adventures."[40] Such a question could only occur to an author interested not in how his works relate to the world

---

34 Xenophon, *Memorabilia*, 3.10.3.
35 Xenophon, *Memorabilia*, 3.10.7.
36 See Kearney, "As If It Were True."
37 Xenophon, *Memorabilia*, 3.10.5.
38 This charming tale of a "very ordinary and rather silly little man" is sure to be of interest to aspiring metarealists everywhere.
39 Auster's *The Red Notebook: True Stories*, by the way, is not quasi-metareal but as metareal as they come.
40 Auster, *City of Glass*, 198.

sitting in my car listening to sports talk radio. I refuse to even consider moving into a house that doesn't feel like the type I would live in.

Think about sex. In the sphere of sexuality, animals are staunch teleologists. Every sexual act has its aim or purpose. But how low, how degraded does human sexuality become when it limits itself to being a mere means to an end, a tool in the service of reproduction? Or, similarly, how much is lost when sex is seen as the equivalent of scratching an itch? The brilliance of Freud is that he recognizes the oddity of human sexuality, the many strange and startling things we bring to it. What is the aim of a fetish? What is the purpose of a kiss? (For Freud the two are connected.) Why do we dress up and play pretend? What is foreplay? And not merely the acts that fall under that moniker, but the perfumes, the makeup, the ribbons and the ties, the music, the dancing, the fruits and wines and lavish meals? Why the performance? Why the show? Such useless and unnecessary add-ons are so integral to human sexuality that to eliminate them is to eliminate the human element altogether. (Which, incidentally, is what the city being constructed by Socrates and his pals seeks to do.)[18]

The same can be said of all forms of love. Love is and must be a love of the useless. Any love that does not transcend transaction is no love at all. I had a student once who took issue with me for insisting that my children are useless. He said that no matter what challenges childrearing poses, kids more than make up for them with chores and yardwork as they grow. Leaving aside that such a perspective could only be offered by someone who has experienced the yardwork end of that bargain and not the raising-and-being-responsible-for-another-human-person end, it is revealing all the same. What it shows is that we are used to thinking in terms of use. We are accustomed to assessing people—others and ourselves—in terms of how productive they are, what they do for work, what

---

18   See, Beauchard, *City of Man*, 57–62.

and their works will be cast into the fires of punishment."[32] My friend, it seems, had not failed. He had somehow created not an image of a living thing, but a real-life human being, and his punishment was to exist in a world populated by his fancies.

This character—whom, he assured me, did not exist prior to the writing of his novel and is very much a fiction sprung like Athena from the mind of its author—now has a life of his own. Not only has he, the character, authored the aforementioned books, he has published articles and book reviews, endorsed other author's works, penned opinion pieces, sat for interviews, presented at conferences, and secured a full-time faculty position at an academic institution of some merit. Like a less sexy, though every bit as seductive, Kelly LeBrock in the 1985 cult classic *Weird Science*, he has become a real human being.

Outlandish? A work of fiction? The mad ravings of an unsound mind? Well, my friend the novelist is a reputable author with multiple titles to his name, but if you won't trust him, perhaps you'll trust some of the western tradition's most esteemed thinkers. In an essay critical of my reading of Plato, the academic philosopher Jean-Luc Beauchard accuses me of arguing that "the kind of art that can get us beyond the postmodern (and its irony and its solipsism and its despair) is the kind that can create new and noble *characters*, that can bring those characters to life, that believes it can lift them off the page and bring them into the world with 'all the inner parts' and 'motion, soul, and wisdom' of real human beings."[33] This exceedingly charming idea, attributed to me by Beauchard, is not my own—though I wish I could take credit for it. And while Beauchard's essay has convinced me that it can be gleaned in the works of Plato, I do not believe it to have originated with him either. Better, I think, to attribute it to some still

---

32   Borges, *Collected Fictions*, 297.
33   Beauchard, "Who is the Philosopher King?," 280.

they offer to society, how much they benefit us. But I do not want to be loved for my use. Nor can I be. I am not my job. I am not my societal role. I am more than what I am good for. We love our IPhones because they benefit us, and when they break, we throw them away. But I do not want to be thrown away when I am no longer useful. (That we do, as a society, throw people away when they no longer conform to the uses we ascribe to them is obvious to anyone who has spent time in a nursing home.) I want to be loved simply because I am, independent of whatever benefit I have to offer. If I loved my children because they were useful, if I measured their worth by what chores they did around the house or even by how much happiness they brought me, I wouldn't love them at all.

Desire, then, is that which distinguishes us from the animal, that which makes us human by freeing us from the bonds of necessity and allowing us to step forth into the light of the useless. Only that which is useless can be valued, valued not in terms of what it does but what it is, valued in and of itself. Yet we said above that desire is that which makes us sick. The root of the uniquely human malady, the cause of our neurosis, is the fact that we exist beyond purpose, that, contrary to Angelus Silesius's oft-quoted poem, it is not the rose but the human being that blooms *without why*. Camus rightly insists that "the meaning of life is the most urgent of questions" and then goes on to conclude that life lacks meaning, that the best we human beings can do is fight on in the face of a sterile, meaningless existence. And while much of his assessment is apt, the thing he fails to note is that it is precisely the ambivalent nature of desire that makes a meaningless existence both a blessing and a curse. Existing without meaning means existing without limitations. Unlike the animal or mineral, bare life or lifeless rock, I cannot be defined. I am beyond definition. Desire frees me from a meaning that is not my own. And yet what could be more painful than to lack purpose? Is there anything more degrading,

say, autumn of 2022 on) my friend claims not to have gone a single week without seeing at least one person wearing a medical mask with skeleton teeth drawn on it.

When he shared these unusual occurrences, I assured him that chance and coincidence play outsized roles in human affairs and advised him not to put much stock in either. "Remember Boethius," I said, "who taught us to see fate as fickle and accidents as occurring without why." (This, of course, is not what Boethius taught, but my friend was disturbed, and I know of no better balm than to cite ancient wisdom, especially to those who neglect Ignatius J. Reilly's sage advice to steep oneself in it.) "I haven't told you the whole story," was his reply.

Apparently, one morning he boarded an empty subway car on his way to work. He sat down. He crossed his legs. He looked to his right and noticed a book on the seat next to him. Recognizing the image on its charming blue cover as an etching by Dalí, he decided to pick it up. What a fateful decision that turned out to be. Its title surprised him. The name of its author shook him to his core. He set the book down, rose to his feet, and exited at the next stop. He walked the rest of the way to work in the rain. He had no umbrella.

When he got to his office, he paced about and debated how frightened he ought to be. It's not every day that an author discovers a book authored by one of his characters. Yes, that's right, the very academic philosopher about whom my friend had written an entire novel was now publishing his own books. More terrifying still, the book in question appears in my friend's unpublished novel, as does another work which is apparently also in print. Borges opens his "Covered Mirrors" with the following words of warning: "Islam tells us that on the unappealable Day of Judgement, all who have perpetrated images of living things will reawaken with their works, and will be ordered to blow life into them and they will fail, and they

anything more perverse, than living a life in the pursuit of nothing at all?

The problem of desire, the problem posed by desire, is that desire is aimless and thus cannot be fulfilled. Unlike need, which can be satiated, which is done away with once one finds a means of providing for what one lacks, desire is insatiable. It only wants *more*. It is, to return to Socrates' question in *Charmides*, a desire for desire itself. One of the fundamental problems of politics—a problem which each successive generation seems less equipped even to recognize, let alone address—is rooted in the conflation of need with desire. The Marxist revolutionary and the Neo-Liberal capitalist suffer from the same deficient understanding of the human person, an understanding that Dostoevsky's underground man disposed of more than a century and a half ago. (Of course, who has time to read Russian literature when there are ideological adversaries to tar?) According to the underground man, no amount of material comfort will do. Even if the social programmers were able to build for me a crystal palace in which all of my needs could be met, still, he insists, I would choose "destruction and chaos" and even "suffering" over living therein, simply because "that is my desire."

> [M]an is a frivolous and unaccountable creature, and perhaps, like a chess-player, he is only fond of the process of achieving his aim, but not of the aim itself. And who knows (it is impossible to be absolutely sure about it), perhaps the whole aim mankind is striving to achieve on earth merely lies in this incessant process of achievement, or (to put it differently) in life itself, and not really in the attainment of any goal, which, needless to say, can be nothing else but twice-two-makes-four, that is to say, a formula; but twice-two-makes-four is not life, gentlemen. It is the beginning of death.[19]

Of course, desire too is the beginning of death and the underground man—who is himself plagued by that

---

19   Dostoevsky, *Notes from the Underground*, 222–225.

tribulations. Set in a city reminiscent of the one in which we live, this gothic novel overlapped with real life in ways apparent to those who know how to look for them. In the work, the philosopher—like all philosophers, I suppose—had reason to doubt his sanity. He became oddly obsessed with numbers and certain astrological signs, tarot cards in particular. I read a draft of the work, and it was fine—its author had produced no *Finnegan's Wake,* and I doubt he'd mind me saying so—but I told people it was alright, if a bit derivative, and I even admitted that I enjoyed it.

In any event, a few years passed, and I had forgotten the work entirely, until one day when I serendipitously ran into my friend at a local diner. I asked him what happened with the book, and he told me he had decided to hold off on publishing it. "It's not that bad," I lied, hoping to inspire a bit of confidence. "You could always self-publish if there are no small indie presses out there willing to take it." But it wasn't the quality of the work, he said, that made him reticent. No, far from it. In fact, he believed the novel to be one of his best. "Well then why not put it out into the world?" I asked. That's when he told me he had experienced several *aberrations* (his word) that caused him to question the divide between life and literature. For instance, one morning on a stroll about town, he noticed that someone had discarded a deck of tarot cards in a nearby gutter. He walked over to take a closer look. This was odd, he thought, but odder still was the card on top staring at him with a crooked smile. It was the Fool—the very card that plays a central role in his book.

That's not all. Another recurring motif in the novel is the idea that we all wear masks to disguise who and what we are. To underscore this, one of the work's more sinister characters begins donning a strange skull mask, a memento mori if you will, meant to reveal that which we'd prefer not to see. The book was written before the pandemic—which, in hindsight, makes it seem almost prophetic—but in the latter years of the COVID crisis (from,

uniquely human disease, hence his: "I am a sick man"—knows it. It is no accident that he pairs destruction, chaos, and suffering with his image of human life.

As Socrates notes, the "feverish city"—that is, the city in which we find ourselves, civilization, rife as it is with the ills of social living—arises out of desire, is born of our lust for unnecessary pleasures (*Republic*, 372e). It is, he says, our futile attempts to satiate our insatiable appetites that cause strife within our cities by causing factions that feud with one another (*Republic*, 470b–e). It is our greed for "unlimited acquisition," our willingness to overstep "the boundary of the necessary" in pursuit of unnecessary desires, that causes us to take up arms and go to war with our neighbors (*Republic*, 373d–e). To quote Camus, "The plague is born of excess. It is excess itself, and has no limits."[20]

Desire, then, is both that which humanizes and, at the very same time, that which dehumanizes. Look to the examples offered above. Each of the useless pleasures that distinguishes me from my animal counterpart is also a form of vice. Gluttony, sloth, lust, greed—which deadly sin isn't connected with desire, which isn't just another guise for desire itself? Elsewhere I have argued that the Eros of Freud is simply Thanatos by another name. Desire is the death-drive. My insatiable appetite for *more* cannot but lead to destruction—be it the destruction of others who stand between me and my desires or the self-destruction that comes from me giving myself over to my desires. The danger of desire, then, for both society and the individual is *the* political problem. All other problems stem from it. But how should we address this danger? Can desire be reined in, can it be managed, without sacrificing the human person thereby?

~

---

20   Camus, "Les Cahiers de la Pléiade."

the only emotion we feel toward the fictive—that is, *created*, though just as real as you and me—characters who populate our lives.

My second epiphany of the metareal highlights just this point. It was recounted to me by my wife who works as a marriage and family therapist. She had been seeing a client for several years, an adolescent girl who found it difficult to make friends. In the absence of much human connection, this young bibliophile threw herself into books. She read voraciously and found herself getting swept up in the stories. Now what she was reading at the time, I cannot remember, but let us say that it was Dickens' *A Christmas Carol*. In fact, it was *A Christmas Carol*. Of this, I'm quite certain. For she recognized something of her own image in the scene from Scrooge's childhood in which he, as a young boy, spent a lonely Christmas holiday with Ali Baba and Robin Crusoe. That we find ourselves in works of fiction ought not to surprise us. What, after all, could be more fictive than the stories we tell ourselves about ourselves and especially about one another? Yet there was something peculiar about this girl's attachment to the characters in Dickens' charming little book. For, being from a devout family and taught from her earliest youth to pray for the souls in Purgatory, she was mortified to learn that Jacob Marley had no hope of escaping his ghostly perdition. The thought tormented her, so acute was her sympathy, and she spent nine consecutive nights on her knees praying a novena for Marley's salvation.

If this story strikes you as unbelievable, then you will likely doubt the veracity of the tale I am about to tell, my third and final illustration of what is meant by metarealism. I swear to you, however, that I experienced it in reality and if you allow yourself to entertain it as true, you too will come to appreciate the power of the metareal. It happened like this. A friend of mine, a novelist, was working on a book about an academic philosopher who leaves the academy and finds himself in the midst of some harrowing

The construction of the city in the *Republic* has as its stated aim the purgation of everything luxurious, all that is unnecessary (*Republic*, 399e). Desire, we have seen, is that which makes us human by allowing us to move above our bare needs into the realm of the unnecessary. But human beings are sick, dangerous creatures whose competing desires pose continuous threats to their own security and the security of others. Thus it should come as no surprise that Socrates' program for achieving social stability and cohesion is to purge the city of desire by bringing its citizenry back down to the level of need. In the pages of the *Republic*, we witness a radical reduction of the human being, a systematic reversion that brings the human person back to the state and status of the animal. (It is not accidental that Socrates and his interlocutors continuously refer to the citizens of their *polis* as cattle, sheep, swine, dogs, etc.)[21] Step by step, the *Republic*'s regime carves from man the very things that make him human. Yet before we criticize such a move—and, indeed, there is much to criticize—we must first understand it. Only once we have identified both *why* and *how* Socrates offers such prescriptions for the ills of the city can we assess whether the *polis* of the *Republic* represents an ideal city—one to be hoped for—or makes plain civilization as it actually is.

Now the *why* is easy enough to address. As our foregoing discussion has shown, desire is the disease. It is, to use Kierkegaard's language, the sickness unto death, a sickness that festers, that makes foul everything it touches, even when it fails to kill. And, paradoxically, the very thing in need of remedy—society—is itself both the cause and the symptom of its ailment. If desire is the neurosis of the city, the city is to blame. If civilization makes man sick, it is the very sickness with which he is infected.

---

21   See, Beauchard, *City of Man*, 33–35. (Notice that I freely cite Beauchard in spite of the unwarranted criticisms he has leveled against my work.)

This is no idealism. In fact, it is more materialist than materialism, reversing the perceived causality between matter and ideas but insisting that ideas are real because they are enfleshed, incarnated in the material world. Don Quixote and Sancho Panza are no mere phantoms. They live and walk among us. Or if not them any more—how few devotees they have today!—then other equally fictive creations. Three anecdotes, recounted by degree of metareality from least to greatest, will serve to illustrate the point. First, I went with my family on a trip to Disney World. While such resorts are replete with examples of man's metareal capacities—whole worlds are invented for the express purpose of offering delight—they are not themselves metareal, but self-consciously "unreal," providing entertainment in the form of fantasy. (Metarealism, remember, insists that for human beings there is no distinction between life and art.) Nevertheless, it is possible to observe—and, indeed, I did observe—metareal moments even in places marked by make-believe.

One such occurrence came in conversation with a young Star Wars fan who told my eldest son and me that he cried when, on a recent episode of one of the dozens of Star Wars spinoffs, his favorite character died. (Full disclosure, I've never been big on Star Wars—what it lacks in plot and character depth, it doesn't do nearly enough to make up for in spectacle and violence—and so I don't remember what show or whose death he was talking about.) The point here is not to question why art affects us as it does—sorry Augustine—but to observe that its effects are the same as those produced by other life events because, of course, aesthetic experiences are life events and all life events are works of art. The grief felt at the loss of a favorite character on a mediocre TV show is every bit as real as the grief felt at the loss of a friend. One can be interpreted as having a greater intensity, depending upon how mediocre the show (or, for that matter, the friend), but the reality of both is inviolable. And grief is far from

Allow me to elaborate. Anyone who wishes to understand social life will inevitably find himself confronted by the question *why society?* Why do human beings live and work together? There is, of course, one answer that jumps readily to mind. A city "comes into being because each of us isn't self-sufficient but is in need of much. . . . Since many things are needed, many men gather in one settlement as partners and helpers" (*Republic*, 369b). Need, then, is the catalyst behind social living. Lack is the reason we form communities. By remaining within the confines of society, I ensure (or at least attempt to ensure) that my needs will be met, that I will have a means of confronting my lack.

But human beings are resourceful animals. We are good at devising ways of meeting our needs. So good, in fact, that when we work together we soon find that we have more than met our needs. Society, then, is the overcoming of society. A partnership that was established in order to address lack not only addresses but eradicates it. Society transcends need. It is the self-overcoming of need, the transformation of need into abundance.[22] And once we have provided for our necessities, we find ourselves wanting *more*. Abundance proves lacking. Enough is never enough. Civilization is discontented precisely because it is civilized. Society is sick because it meets our needs and thus points a way beyond them. In the *Republic*, "the city of utmost necessity" devolves into the "feverish city" (or, as Freud would have it, the neurotic city) as a matter of course. From the moment the city is founded, it harbors

---

22 Abundance, of course, does not mean abundance for all. The absurdity of human affairs is never more apparent than when one considers how a society with the means of meeting its citizenry's needs invents ways not to meet them because the desires of some trump the needs of others. Think, for example, of the Agricultural Adjustment Act passed during the Great Depression, which, at a time when people were literally starving to death, paid farmers to slaughter their cattle and not plant crops. Such insanities, it goes without saying, persist to this day.

ing up unrealities, it is Unamuno's contention that some do in fact impose their dreams upon existence. In a work that anticipates Borges to such a degree that one wonders if the Tiresias of Buenos Aires might have written it and then ascribed it to a character of his own invention—Unamuno is a proto-Menard if ever there was one—the author enters into his novel as a character, one among many, in order to dissuade one of his characters from committing suicide. But, as the *nivola* itself proclaims, "Characters often end up toying with their author" and the plan goes to pieces.[28] Instead of Unamuno consoling the book's protagonist, Augusto Pérez, he is confronted by Pérez and forced to admit that he himself may be a work of fiction, the mad creation of some Cartesian evil genius, some infinite Leibniz working in obscurity and self-effacement, who has a whole chorus of characters at his disposal, doing God knows what, playing a very intricate and subtle game.

"Haven't you said," Pérez presses Unamuno, "that Don Quixote and Sancho are not just as real but even more real than Cervantes?"[29] And of course, Unamuno has said this—more than once.[30] The odd thing, however, is that he's right. Like Borges' unnamed sorcerer, Unamuno realizes that dreaming "a fully-fleshed man" is "not impossible, though it was clearly supernatural."[31] That human beings have this supernatural ability is known to every metarealist—that is, the great authors and artists of existence who have dared to dream reality rather than acquiesce to it. Metarealism, you see, recognizes that while an individual lives in himself, his inventions belong to the world and are the fabric from which the world is made.

28　Unamuno, *Fog*, 90.
29　Unamuno, *Fog*, 160.
30　See, for instance, "Our knight was a reasonable lunatic; he was not a fictious creature, as the worldings believe, but a man who has eaten and drunk, slept and died." Unamuno, *Life of Don Quixote and Sancho*, 34. Cf. Unamuno, *The Tragic Sense of Life*, 187–205.
31　Borges, *Collected Fictions*, 97–98.

within itself the seeds of its own destruction. Its citizens will soon have enough (and more than enough) and will subsequently demand more and more and ever more (see, *Republic*, 373d–373e).

How can society address the problem that society has created? What remedy can society offer to the illness that society is? This, I would argue, is the chief concern of the *Republic*, the task that Plato sets out to answer. At first glance, there seems to be no way out of this quagmire. Civilization appears of necessity to entail its own ruin. But further consideration reveals that the illness and the remedy are one. The very city that makes men sick by raising them above the level of need cures them by reducing them back to it. It is by implementing a regime that prevents people—if not all, then certainly most—from moving into the realm of desire that society secures its own foundations. This is why Socrates famously defines justice as each citizen doing his one job. For, so long as everyone focuses on fulfilling just "one of the functions in the city" and nothing more, everyone will do only what is necessary (*Republic*, 433a). No one will desire what another has or want to do what another does because each will embody justice as "the practice of minding one's own business" (*Republic*, 433b).

Of course, this reduction of the human being back to the animal comes at a price. But that price is paid by the individual, not the city. (As one ardent defender of civilized society so eloquently put it: Better that the individual die than the nation perish.) The question, then, is not whether society should treat its citizens like swine (*Republic*, 372d)—it already does and, indeed, must if it is going to survive (cf. *Republic*, 343b–d; 459a–e)—the question is how society can accomplish so great and difficult a task. By what means can it secure itself against the threat posed by the desire of its citizens? How can it get the genie back into the bottle? And here the *Republic* offers a startling answer—startling, in part, because of how thoroughly mis-

tion). There are truths *out there* which "are the case" and a gulf exists between them and the unreality of artistic creation. Nietzsche reverses this binary. Recasting the tragic stage as the navel of the world, the altar where God enters the frame and reveals himself in all his Dionysian glory, Nietzsche insists that the agony and exuberance expressed in and through art give voice to "our innermost being, our common ground."[25] It is daily life that is imitative, a mere construction, an artistic illusion, "the reflection of suffering, primal and eternal, the sole ground of the world: the 'mere appearance' here is the reflection of eternal contradiction, the father of things."[26]

This dichotomy—which, of course, is operative in Plato, to whom every idea owes some recognition—is so farcical that one wonders if its creator offered it in jest. And yet, as Albertus Secundus says, by treating such inanities as true, serious and conscientious people make it so that *enti nascendique facultati paululum appropinquant.* In a sense, this is metarealism at its finest. That which is not *is* because we take it to be so. An idea has become a reality. More than that, it has become the precondition of every other reality, from the tree outside my window to the desk at which I sit to your individual person to my own. Recognizing this means acknowledging man's ability to fashion existence out of thought, creating the world through concepts. The implications are immense. I will leave it to the lawmakers and social scientists to elucidate what this means for practical living. A few literary examples will suit my purposes here.

In "The Circular Ruins," Borges tells the story of a man who "wanted to dream a man. He wanted to dream him completely, in painstaking detail, and impose him upon reality."[27] A fantastical thought? Not if Miguel de Unamuno is to be believed. For, while all of us are capable of dream-

---

25   Nietzsche, *The Birth of Tragedy*, 81.
26   Nietzsche, *The Birth of Tragedy*, 84.
27   Borges, *Collected Fictions*, 97.

read the text has been on this very point, the most fundamental point in the book. *Reason*. Reason, the *Republic* tells
us, is the tool by which civilization reduces man to beast.
Reason, logic, the rational faculty.

In *Against Method*, Feyerabend writes:

> Just as a well-trained pet will obey his master no matter how
> great the confusion in which he finds himself, and no matter
> how urgent the need to adopt new patterns of behaviour, so
> in the very same way a well-trained rationalist will obey the
> mental image of his master, he will conform to the standards
> of argumentation he has learned, he will adhere to these stan-
> dards no matter how great the confusion in which he finds
> himself, and he will be quite incapable of realizing that what
> he regards as the 'voice of reason' is but a causal after-effect
> of the training he had received. He will be quite unable to
> discover that the appeal to reason to which he succumbs so
> readily is nothing but a political manoeuvre.[23]

Feyerabend is a good reader of Plato. Revisit the last line
in particular. There you will find, in a single sentence, the
clearest, most concise articulation of the central thesis
of Plato's masterwork. Reason is a political maneuver, a
means of restricting the desires, restricting them because
they are dangerous . . . to the state. And it does so, as Feyerabend aptly observes, by reducing man to a rational animal, a well-trained pet.

Consider the education of the guardian class in the
Republic. Book IV, in particular, details at length the rear-
ing of the guardian souls, souls which, we are told, have
been trained to obey the dictates of reason: "as a dog is
called back by a shepherd, [so the soul of the guardian]
is called back by the reason within and calmed" (*Republic*, 440d).[24] Strikingly, Glaucon responds to this assertion

---

23 Feyerabend, *Against Method*, 25. I am thankful to Oliver Crayphius
    for pointing me to this citation.
24 Here I rely upon the 1903 Adams rendition of the text because it
    conveys more clearly the meaning intended. For future citations, I
    return to Bloom unless otherwise stated.

which is objectively true. But as our foregoing discussion has attempted to make plain, the very notion that there is a distinction between reality and artistry is itself a work of art. It is an invention of the human mind that conceals, and at times reveals, our creative capacities. Like Parrhasius' curtain, it deceives many and enlivens a few.[22] Great artists have always taken their calling from it. Ask them what task stands before them. None would dare blaspheme against the muses by saying that their works are pretend. They create for real, and their creations are as real as you and me. They birth art as we birth children. And like children, their art is the future. It will one day grow up and remake the world in its image. As Plutarch so rightly observes, καὶ τὰ μηκέτ' ὄντα τῷ μνημονεύειν ἐναργῶς, ὄντα ποιοῦσιν ἑαυτοῖς.[23]

The same devotion is rarely found among the philosophers, though their offspring can be just as inventive. Consider the two most significant works on poetic imagination in the western tradition, Aristotle's *Poetics* and Nietzsche's *The Birth of Tragedy*. Both approach the veil of Parrhasius, and both fail to recognize it as such. For Aristotle, art is imitation. It takes a reality, a thing in the world, and re-presents it either accurately or, as is often the case, altered. "The poet, like a painter or any other image-maker, is engaged in representation, and there are three kinds of thing that he is representing: things that are or were the case, things that are said or thought to be the case, and things that ought to be the case."[24] Art imitates life. It does not invent it (though the subtle reader will no doubt fix his attention on the third kind of representa-

22 I like to think of Zeuxis, upon discovering Parrhasius' ingenious trick, going back to work on his own painting, in the hopes of improving the child, and attracting birds, artists, and admirers anew. Perhaps he was so inspired and invigorated by the work that he spent the rest of his days perfecting it.

23 "They [the wise] bring even those things that don't exist into being by thinking of them vividly." Plutarch, *De Tranqualitate Animi*, 437c. (I am grateful to my friend, Professor Joaquim Nivola, for helping me translate this fine passage).

24 Aristotle, *Poetics*, 1460b.

by noting that the guardians themselves have, through-out the conversation, been likened to "dogs obedient to the rulers, who are like shepherds of a city" and Socrates replies, "You have a fine understanding of what I want to say" (*Republic*, 440d). What Socrates wants to say is that while some souls are "trimmed in earliest childhood" (*Republic*, 519a), "maimed," as it were, by their indoctrination into the cult of reason (the noble lie of education) which turns man into "a swinish beast" (*Republic*, 535e), others—the rulers—are allowed to leave their desire fully intact. But more on this in the pages to come. For now, let us emphasize that it is the "calculating part" of the soul—reason—that is introduced as a means of constraining and restricting desire (*Republic*, 441e) and that the chief goal of training people to be rational is to protect society from the desires of its citizenry.

Indeed, what can be trusted more than a well-trained dog? But even an untrained dog is predictable and thus preferable to a human being. In spite of the traditional definition—a definition which, our argument now leads us to suspect, may have been offered in bad faith—man is not distinguished from his animal brethren by reason. No, every animal is a rational animal. Rational self-interest is the driving force behind all life. What distinguishes man, as we have said, is not his ability to follow necessary means to a necessary end (Spinoza's dictates of reason). What distinguishes man is *desire*—the drive to follow unnecessary means to no end at all. And, while Socrates is convinced—and convinces us—that by cultivating reason as a safeguard against desire we will live "according to nature" (*Republic*, 444d), human beings, we must admit, are the most unnatural of animals—and that is precisely the thing that sets us apart.

~

A curtain, drawn with such singular truthfulness, that Zeuxis, elated with the judgment which had been passed upon his work by the birds, haughtily demanded that the curtain should be drawn aside to let the picture be seen. Upon finding his mistake, with a great degree of ingenuous candour he admitted that he had been surpassed, for that whereas he himself had only deceived the birds, Parrhasius had deceived him, an artist.

This, then—the curtain of Parrhasius—is the image that most exemplifies the metareal understanding of human existence. For, while the curtain may deceive, it also serves as the occasion by which the artist awakens from his dogmatic slumber and recognizes the ubiquity of art. The painted veil both conceals art's place at the foundation of experience and, when attended to more closely, reveals it.[20] It is the veil drawn by us over everything. And yet, it is no veil at all. For, behind it is nothing, and it alone constitutes our reality.[21]

Human life, that is, is rooted in an elaborate *trompe-l'œil*, one which has been assumed by us from the start and which grounds the reality of every other artistic creation. We divide the world into two categories—truth and appearance, the real and the artificial, the natural and the manmade. There is a world, we say, outside our world, a real world, not dependent upon our perception of it, one

20   As Pliny tells us of the genius of Parrhasius: "To paint substantial bodies and the interior of objects is a great thing, no doubt, but at the same time it is a point in which many have excelled: but to make the extreme outline of the figure, to give the finishing touches to the painting in rounding off the contour, this is a point of success in the art which is but rarely attained. For the extreme outline, to be properly executed, requires to be nicely rounded, and so to terminate as to prove the existence of something more behind it, and thereby disclose that which it also serves to hide."

21   "Art . . . is a veil, rather than a mirror. She has flowers that no forests know of, birds that no woodland possesses. She makes and unmakes many worlds . . . Hers are the 'forms more real than living man,' and hers the great archetypes of which things that have existence are but unfinished copies." Wilde, *The Decay of Lying*, 21.

The city as we have described it is, we must admit, a thoroughly masculine affair. The old Augustinian moniker *city of man* can be understood in its narrowest sense to describe a *polis* so constructed, a city that prizes reason over desire—reason to the exclusion of desire—necessity over caprice, order over life itself. In some ways, that is to be expected. The *Republic* is, after all, a dialogue authored by a man in which eleven male interlocutors from a thoroughly patriarchal society discuss politics. What is more, it is no secret that the history of philosophy has often neglected the feminine, feared it, suppressed it, relegated it to the realm of the irrational and untrue. Yet in Book V, Socrates makes a striking admission. Everything described prior to that point, he says, has merely been a "male drama." And "having completely finished the male drama," the time has come "to complete the female" (*Republic*, 451c).

When I teach the *Republic*, my students—who, like all of us, are products of the age and thus assume its ideals—gravitate to Book V. Socrates, they say, is laudably progressive. His call for the education of women, his recognition of the natural equality of the sexes, his belief that women too can and should take part in matters of state,[25] make him an almost unheralded pioneer of the women's rights movement. His only fault is that he comes too soon, arrives on the scene two and a half millennia too early. If we today have yet to fully realize his revolutionary vision, that is because we still fail to see that society as it is structured is "against nature" (*Republic*, 456c), that our roles are merely constructs, that we have been trained to see difference where no essential difference lies.

Unfortunately, such readings bring more to the text than they take from it. Remember, for Socrates, returning us to our natural state is returning us to the level of the

---

25 To say nothing of what he would have us do with the unwanted fetuses in the *polis* (461c). See Beauchard's commentary on this and related passages in *City of Man*, 58–62.

to the greatness of human artistic achievement. We have divided up the cosmos and refashioned it so convincingly that, to quote Razumikhin without citation, we lie and then go on believing our own lies. Or at least this is what the great artists have done for us—given us a world in which to live, a comprehensible world we take to be our own. A long-neglected image will help to elucidate the point. In the 36th chapter of the 35th book of Pliny the Elder's *Naturalis Historia*, we are presented with the story of Zeuxis, the famous Greek painter known for his ability to produce lifelike works of art. Having painted a portrait of a child carrying a bowl of lush white grapes, Zeuxis is dismayed to spot a dimwitted gaggle of birds pecking at the fruit. "I have surely painted the grapes better than the child," he laments. "For if I had fully succeeded in the last, the birds would have been in fear of it and flown away."

This wonderful anecdote, and the embellishments that improve upon it, have provided much fodder for scholars and artists in recent years. But, as Socrates tells Gorgias, Zeuxis is not the world's only painter, and, as Cervantes notes, to focus exclusively on him is to buy into his slanders.[19] Consider, then, another tale, one found, like a cloud, hovering just above Zeuxis and his birds. The great artist-hero Parrhasius—the significance of whose name ought not to be overlooked—challenged Zeuxis to a contest. It takes an exceptional painter, he knew, to attract the attention of free flying birds, capable as they are of going where they will. So he devised a little bird trap of his own. What did he produce?

---

19 See Plato, *Gorgias*, 453c–d and Cervantes, *Don Quixote*, 26, respectively. While the latter passage is typically read as referring to Zoilus as the libeler and Zeuxis as the painter, our interpretation pairs with Pliny's assertion that "Zeuxis had stolen the art from others and had taken it all to himself"—which, after all, is the aim of slander—and returns the literary theorist to his rightful place as painter of new worlds.

animal. It is precisely the *unnatural* that makes us human. Thus, to educate female guardians alongside their male counterparts is not to emancipate them but to reduce them along with the men to useful tools, predictable animals that can be trusted to do society's bidding.

> "Do we believe the females of the guardian dogs must guard the things the males guard along with them and hunt with them, and do the rest in common; or must they stay indoors as though they were incapacitated as a result of bearing and rearing the puppies, while the males work and have all the care of the flock?"
>
> "Everything in common," he said ...
>
> "Is it possible," I said, "to use any animal for the same things if you don't assign it the same rearing and education?"
>
> "No, it's not possible."
>
> "If, then, we use the women for the same things as the men, they must also be taught the same things" (*Republic*, 451d–e).

Men and women—"both animals" (*Republic*, 455d)—are, according to Socrates, equally capable of contributing to society and securing its foundations. Neither, then, ought to be neglected. Both can be put to use; both become pawns in the hands of a civilized regime. What is more, if we fail to educate women, then we fail to educate the desire out of them. Men cannot be allowed to have a monopoly on reason because female desire is as dangerous to the social order as male desire—perhaps even more so. No, everyone must be stripped of *his or her* humanity, a stripping made explicit when we are told that the women in Socrates' ideal city will be made to exercise "naked with the men in the palaestras" (*Republic*, 452b).

We said above that Book V is where the male drama gives way to the female, and now we find not an affirmation of female desire but a degrading of the female to the same hyper-rational, quasi-animal state of men in the *polis*. In

be depended upon. An object whose existence has been proved and, when we're truly enjoying the scent of our own flatus, proved *scientifically*. We take its being as independent of our own. We consider it part of the real world.

In assuming this, we fail to appreciate that the "real world" is our own invention, made up of "independent" "facts" of our own creation. We see existence as something that can be divided into parts, parts which just so happen to correspond to the categories we use to decipher them. (What luck!) The predicament is made clearer still if we consider beings that preexist or are not manufactured by us. A tree, for instance. What makes this oak in my backyard, the one my kids love to climb and play on, a single tree, distinct from the totality of the universe? Who decided it was a tree and not something else? (And please spare me your Phil 100 lecture on "treeness," as if that solves anything.) The tree is a tree because we—the artists of existence—declare it so.[17] Apart from us, there is no tree. There is life coursing through existence. But existence is existence. (Or rather, not even that—a purblind potency discernable to none.) We are the ones who, by means of imagination, break it down and name the abstracted parts.[18]

What is the cause of this amnesia about the artistry of man? How have we forgotten our essential character? I suspect that this lapse in memory is in part attributable

---

17 There are readers, I suspect, who will be put off by this, though I doubt they can refute it. They will want to attribute the creation of the tree—and even, *Kyrie eléison*, treeness—to the divine artist. Before fielding such objections, I would simply point our naysaying friends to *Genesis* 2:19. Funny how scripture contradicts our most piously held beliefs—when we bother to read it.

18 As Oscar Wilde notes in his remarkable *The Decay of Lying*, "Nature is no great mother who has borne us. She is our creation. It is in our brain that she quickens to life. Things are because we see them, and what we see, and how we see it, depends on the arts that have influenced us. To look at a thing is very different from seeing a thing. One does not see anything until one sees its beauty. Then, and then only, does it come into existence."

what way, then, does Book V represent a transition away from the masculine structure that came before? What shift allows us to call this a "female" drama? The answer, I think, lies in an insult leveled against Plato's Socrates by Alcibiades: "you're quite a flute-player, aren't you?" (*Symposium*, 215b). Anyone who reads enough of the dialogues will begin to notice certain recurring themes, themes that never seem to be mentioned in the traditional readings of the texts. One, for instance, is how vitally important it is both to be handsome and to surround oneself with other handsome people (*Republic*, 494c; *Symposium*, 194d; *Charmides*, 154b–e; *Meno.* 67b–c; 80c; etc.). Another is how immoral it is to play the flute (*Republic*, 561c; *Protagoras*, 347c–e; *Philebus*, 56a; *Alcibiades*, 106e).[26] The *Symposium*, you will remember, begins with the expulsion of the flute girl (*Symposium*, 176e), an expulsion which, I have argued elsewhere, signals the exclusion of female desire from the conversation on eros at the all-male drinking party. In the *Republic*, both the flute makers and the flute players find themselves banished from the city (*Republic*, 399d). Why such animus? What did flute playing do to deserve Plato's ire?

The flute, Socrates tells us, is "panharmonic"—that is, not simple, orderly, and harmonious in the way that, say, a lyre is, but rather unruly, improvisational, Dionysian (to use Nietzsche's language). It is "the most many-stringed" instrument (*Republic*, 399d), capable of captivating its listeners, enflaming their unconscious desires, encouraging them to give themselves over to it and be led by it like a marionette dangling from its strings (cf. *Republic*, 411a–b). It is dangerous because it is the instrument of Marsyas, not Apollo (*Republic*, 399e), the instrument of revelry, drunkenness, and excess, not modesty, orderliness, and mod-

---

26 Nietzsche, who, as I noted above, understood Plato and the games he played well enough to want to get in on the joke, also has some derogatory things to say about flute playing. See *Beyond Good and Evil*, §186.

import, the suggestion seems to be that, in the absence of human consciousness, the oneness of the world would remain intact. Or, said differently, human beings make multiplicity where unity is.

Consider any one being, say, the desk at which I presently sit. What distinguishes this desk from the floor on which it rests, the wall it is backed up against, the objects strewn haphazardly upon it—my laptop, my lamp, countless pens, pictures of my wife and kids, ungraded assignments (now long overdue), stacks upon stacks of books and stray notepads, an old coffee mug with grounds dried up at the bottom, a seemingly out-of-place icon of St. Thérèse, you get the idea—what distinguishes it from the room in which it dwells, the house in which that room resides, the plot of land on which that house is built, the street, the town, the state, the country, the continent, the hemisphere, the world, the totality of being? The answer, I think, is clear. What differentiates my desk is *me*. Or, to speak more correctly, my mind. I separate this single object out from the unity of existence and bring it forth into the light of consciousness like Descartes with his wax. The "desk" is an abstraction, created by me in order to help me navigate and interpret an otherwise oceanic (and thus overwhelming) cosmos.[16]

Does this mean that the *principium individuationis* is mere illusion? Not at all. Nothing could be more real. Singularity and multiplicity are the heart of human existence. The problem is that in our eagerness to smash up the universe and recreate it as we deem fit—for destruction and creation always go hand in hand—we lose sight of the fact that we're the ones doing the dividing. We forget that "the desk" is not "the desk" for anyone but us and take our own artistry for an unchangeable law of the universe. "The desk," we say, is a reality. It is a solid thing. A fact to

---

16　As Montaigne, ever wiser than we are, rightly notes, "We have done right to emphasize our imaginative powers: all our goods exist only in a dream." *An Apology for Raymond Sebond*, 54.

eration. Well then, what are we to make of the fact that Socrates—that stoical old moralizer—is accused of playing the flute? What are we to make of it that Alcibiades compares him to Marsyas himself (*Symposium*, 215c)? Is Socrates not, if we are being honest, very much like a pied piper, charming the youths of Athens with his charming little tune (cf. *Phaedo* 60d–61c; 77e–78b)?

Book V is the central book of the *Republic* both literally—coming precisely at the center of the ten-book work—and metaphorically—containing the work's most central idea: the rule of the philosopher king. It is a turning point where the dialogue's focus shifts from a conversation on the nature of justice to a conversation on the nature of philosophy and, more to the point, the philosopher *herself*. I change pronouns here intentionally because if from Book V on the *Republic* becomes a female drama, it does so with the philosopher as its leading lady. Unlike the other citizens of the *polis*—those thoroughly masculine rationalists who, as we have seen, are robbed of their desire and thus reduced to a more natural, animal state—the philosopher—who is "erotic," "insatiable," "a desirer of wisdom" (*Republic*, 475a–d)—the philosopher alone is allowed to be "unnatural" (*Symposium*, 219c). She alone can be a flute girl, indulging her passions, pursuing her desire, pursuing it in the extreme, enjoying that sweet human lust for more and ever more, that truly erotic impulse to never have enough.[27]

~

Justice in the city is, according to Socrates, nothing more than each person doing his one job, each fulfilling

---

27　Flute girls were young prostitutes who would attend male banquets in ancient Athens in order to provide musical entertainment and sexual pleasure for the guests. See Aristotle, *The Athenian Constitution*, (L,2) and Aristophanes, *Wasps*, lines 1342–1365. I am indebted to John Manoussakis, a talented flute player in his own right, for first bringing this to my attention.

beautiful, seductive muse, worthy of love, reverence, and devotion. It was Scott Fitzgerald who said that the mark of true genius is the ability to hold two contradictory ideas in one's mind and go on living. But the task before us is not to go on living. It is to forge ahead. It is to create. It is to prosper. How are we to do that in light of the lamentations laid out above? If you'll allow me to remain with Plato just a moment longer—I promise, we'll dispense with him soon enough—then I would suggest that we, like he, ask what life is. Whence this mysterious, divine breath breathed into existence, animating everything, from the movement of the heavenly bodies to the particles of particles from which all things are made? In the build up to *Phaedrus'* orgy of innuendo, Socrates attempts to prove the immortality of the soul by showing that the principle of life is unending. That which animates itself and is the cause of animation in others has no cause. It is self-moving. It always has been and always will be.

While many are wont to skip over the philosophical sleight of hand implicit in Socrates' shift from speaking of the life force (all-soul) to individual immortality (every soul), let us linger upon it—for here indeed is a point worth making. The continuity of all life, the oneness of the whole, is indisputable. (How would we even conceive of the whole if it were not one?) We have understood this from the time of the presocratics—think of Thales, "All is water"—and the last few philosophers left today, that is, the physicists, tell us that there is a fixed amount of energy in the universe. What then accounts for the fragmenting of this primal unity? Who set about smashing things up?

Contrary to the philosophically illiterate view so prevalent today that the ancients anthropomorphized the universe, making man the center of all things, the traditional answer to the question of what fractured an otherwise unified existence is—the human soul. Original sin, it seems, predates Augustine. Tabling the moral implications of this assertion and considering merely the phenomenological

the role assigned to him for the benefit of all (*Republic*, 433a). And if we look honestly at the demands of society—the demands that we social creatures place upon one another—we will have to admit that justice understood as such is the law of all social living. When students enter my classroom, they do not want me to be Matthew Clemente the lover or friend, the sufferer, the worrier, the man with a short temper who resembles (to an unsettling degree) his father, the adult child who still feels and acts like a little boy, the self-possessed writer who is desperate for the admiration of others, the frustrated parent who can't seem to get parenting right, the anxious control freak who lays awake all night with tightness in his chest and wonders if he is finally dying or just having another panic attack. No, what they expect—what they demand—is that I be Professor Clemente. What they want is for me to be my job.

To students—and even more so to the university that employs me—I am an expert in my field, someone who has spent a lot of time reading books and thus knows what they say, someone who can articulate clearly what it means to fulfill the core requirement the university has forced upon students and perhaps can show why the university has forced it upon them. The secret, of course, is that what they expect me to be is not what I am. What they expect me to be is the opposite of what I am. Anyone who has read enough to be an expert knows that he is no expert. Anyone who has attempted to understand a book knows that he has no clue what it says. Anyone who has cared enough about philosophy to dedicate his life to it knows that it is utterly useless, cannot benefit students, not in the way they want it to, not in the way they expect it to, pay for it to—not in the way he once thought it could. And anyone who has asked himself *who am I?* knows that he is not one but many, not a static, definable thing but a multitude of urges and impulses, drives and desires coursing and colliding under the skin.

speech in the *Symposium* to a classroom full of under-graduates and winking suggestively as I did so—but the humor is serious business; it is not meant to be taken in jest. Sex, Socrates proposes, stands at the foundation of everything. Desire is the catalyst for the creation of the world. If there is to be life after death, life out of death, it must be birthed into existence by the same spirit that inspires us to give birth, the desire to create ourselves and one another anew and imagine and reimagine life other-wise. This erotic, artistic impulse is difficult to channel, especially in an age that no longer values giving birth, a nihilistic age good at identifying the problems inherent in life but lacking the creativity to be seduced by life, the artistry to make life seductive.

Humor, of course, has an essential role to play in coun-tering this precipitous decline. And at this most self-seri-ous of times, it is up to the philosophers to remind us to take ourselves lightly.[15] But how can we do so when facing the gravest of problems? The first step, I think, is to iden-tify the problems for what they are, name them, and speak honestly about them. Platitudes, vague utterances, aca-demic claptrap, and indirect communication will not do. What is needed is candid discussion and thorough phil-osophical examination. On the topics of death, suffering, meaninglessness, the burdens and constraints of social living, the allure of suicide, the problem of madness, civ-ilization's inability to protect us, the futility of attempting to fulfill the demands of justice, our own inner wretched-ness and the perverse nature of human desire, the frailty of the body and the viciousness of the soul—on the bru-tality of the world and the inhumanity of man, we must speak. These are facts, and we can silence them with our inattention no longer.

And yet, if we are to speak, we must do so while remem-bering that in spite of all this—and perhaps even, in some mysterious, quasi-mystical way, because of it—life is a

---

15   See, Clemente, "Touch Thyself," 207–214.

In *Being and Nothingness*, Sartre offers his famous example of the waiter who is not actually a waiter—not actually anything at all—but becomes one simply by showing up and playing the part. The would-be waiter is not his one job, is not limited to the role it assigns him. He only becomes a waiter when he starts to act like one. Once he begins putting on his show, once the patrons in the café see him dressed up in a waiter's attire, moving hurriedly from table to table, taking down their orders, walking back and forth to the kitchen, carrying their food around the room on his arms—then he is a waiter. It is only by pretending that he becomes what he is. It is by going along with the game, by forgetting that it is a game and, like a good method actor, refusing to give up the part that he placates society and justifies himself.

Now, each of us is a waiter in a café. Each spends his days convincing others that he is defined by and confined to his one job. (Is it an accident that when we meet someone for the first time, we introduce ourselves by saying what it is we *do*?) But in order to deceive others, we must first deceive ourselves. So we play our parts, claim for ourselves the roles that society forces upon us. Before the *polis* has the chance to tell me that I must limit myself to my function, that I must exist as an object to be used by others for the benefit of society itself, I volunteer. I am eager to exist at the level of necessity. I want to be definable, knowable, limited to my use. I want to be rid, once and for all, of the desire to be anything *more*, anything ambiguous, elusive, not a human *being* but a human *becoming*, a transitional creature that cannot be nailed down. That is why I like being a professor, why I liked being called "Professor" (so much so that when some hapless student begins an email with the accurate yet imprecise greeting "Dear Mr. Clemente"—or, horror of horrors, "Dear Matthew"—it has the ability to prejudice me against him forever). Being a professor gives me an identity, a meaning, a way of understanding myself. It

true reader, heir to Theseus, who will hunt him out and wrestle from him his secrets.[14]

This game of hide and seek is, however, more than a game. It is a means of saying what can't be said, approaching the tragedy of existence by way of the comic. I suggested earlier that the art best suited to get us beyond our "gluttonous, overindulged yet never chastened postmodern malaise," as one exceedingly fine writer recently put it, is in some sense similar to the funeral rites of the Christians. In his second speech on erotic love, Socrates offers an example of what that art can be. To begin with, he speaks *in persona Stesi*, not as himself but as another. And yet, paradoxically, he is never more himself than when speaking as another. (That he quite literally conceals himself before making his first, failed speech but uncovers his head, thus revealing his face, before his second indicates as much.) What is more, the myth he offers is transformative, taking the brutal fact of death—which, as *Symposium* 207d makes undeniably clear, is for Socrates a finality—and turning it into something to celebrate, a play to be laughed at. The hilarity of the soul's ascent could only be missed by those who have never told a dirty joke. The messy business of purification, we are informed, is "terribly noisy, very sweaty, and disorderly" (*Phaedrus*, 248b). The heaven-bound soul, as it sprouts wings and ascends toward life everlasting, notices that "the feather shafts swell and rush to grow from their roots . . . [and] the whole soul seethes and throbs in this condition. Like a child whose teeth are just starting to grow in, and its gums are all aching and itching—that is exactly how the soul feels when it begins to grow wings. It swells up and aches and tingles as it grows them" (*Phaedrus*, 251b–c).

The dialogues are rife with such ribald humor—I once got myself into a bit of trouble by reading Agathon's

---

14   And if you would like to know how the wrestling will proceed, be sure to check out *Theaetetus* 169a–b and cf. Aristophanes, *Clouds*, lines 175–180.

rids me of the burden of indeterminacy, chaos, change—
the burden of human existence.

For Socrates, there is no greater threat to the social
order than for individuals to want to be more than the one
thing they are. The "destruction of the city," he says, comes
about when citizens desire to step beyond their narrowly
defined roles (*Republic*, 434b). Anyone who wants to do
another man's job or have another man's things—"covet-
ousness" it used to be called, though today the cheerful
Neo-Liberal calls it ambition—anyone who wants to live
another man's life, to be another man, other than what
he already is, is guilty of committing the most "extreme
evil-doing" (*Republic*, 434c). Of course, Socrates is not
unaware that every man is already another man, each of
us always already double. Just as the doctor is both healer
and poisoner (*Republic*, 332d), the poet both liar and truth
teller (*Republic*, 377a), the philosopher king both just ruler
and unjust tyrant, so too does each of us harbor within
himself a "double man" (*Republic*, 397e); so too does each
of us possess a Gyges-like ability to reveal or conceal our
secret interiorities, our manifold desires, the multiplicity
hidden within.

In Book VIII, where Socrates lays out the devolution of
the city from aristocratic to tyrannic, he criticizes democ-
racy for encouraging citizens to pursue their desires
without distinguishing good from bad, necessary from
unnecessary, useful from harmful (*Republic*, 561c). The
democratic man, he says,

> . . . lives alone day by day, gratifying the desire that occurs
> to him, at one time drinking and listening to the flute, at
> another downing water and reducing; now practicing gym-
> nastic, and again idling and neglecting everything; and
> sometimes spending his time as though he were occupied
> with philosophy. Often he engages in politics and, jumping
> up, says and does whatever chances to come to him . . . And
> there is neither order nor necessity in his life, but calling
> this life sweet, free, and blessed, he follows it throughout
> (*Republic*, 561c–d).

a rebellious posture, and rebellion is always defined from without. Were he remembered only for his irony, Socrates would not be remembered at all. (How many commentators even deign to mention it?) No, what the dialogues offer is another, subtler form of art, one of which the postmodern is utterly unaware.

Turn now to the *Phaedrus*. After recanting his initial condemnation of erotic desire, Socrates offers a second speech in praise of the divine madness of love. Only, according to him, it isn't his speech at all. Now he speaks as "Stesichorus, Euphemus' son, from Himera" (*Phaedrus*, 244a)—that is, leader of the dance, son of the good speaker, from the land of desire. Who, one might ask, is this leader of the dance?[12] (And what the dance? Etymological evidence suggests it consists of crowds of people walking round in a ring. Socrates himself tells us that the best dancers are likewise the best in war.) Who is the dance leader's father, the good speaker? What does it mean to hail from the land of desire? That Socrates should choose to distance himself from himself in order to inhabit various *personae* ought not to surprise us.[13] Part of the Platonic aesthetic is to attribute one's words (and even one's thoughts, desires, and actions) to another. As I have argued elsewhere, the dialogues are nothing if not a labyrinth in which their author hides himself like the minotaur, awaiting the arrival of a

---

12 Richard Kearney, in a provocative reading of this passage, suggests that the choice of the name Stesichorus is Plato's way of nodding to himself "as the one directing the chorus in the Dialogues, all these different characters, a kind of a symphony of voices coming in and playing off of one another." See Kearney, "The Philosophical Poet and the Poetic Philosopher," 232. While I'm not convinced of this, it is certainly interesting to note that the people of Himera, like Plato, sought to overthrow Dionysius I of Syracuse. What to make of that accident of history is a question better left to far subtler readers than I.

13 A similar mask is assumed in the *Symposium* where Diotima of Mantinea provides Socrates with his desired disguise. Interested readers ought to consider the import of her name and place of origin as Kearney charmingly did in our previous footnote.

The dangers associated with encouraging citizens to live thusly have been established at length above. What is of particular interest, however, is how Socrates describes the inner life of this singular man, singular not because he is just one thing but because his many desires belong to him and him "alone" (*Republic*, 561c). "'Well,' I said, 'I suppose that this man is all-various and full of the greatest number of dispositions, the fair and many-colored man'" (*Republic*, 561e).

This all-various man is what each of us is, though none of us seems to know it. (Who among us can resist the pleasures of "drinking and *listening to the flute*"?) He is human, truly human, free from the bonds of necessity, able to pursue his "insatiable desire" without end (*Republic*, 562c). Desire is that which distinguishes him, that which sets him apart. Anyone who has bought into the Socratic ideal—civilized society's ideal—of *one man, one job* only to lose his job has had to face the fact that he has always been replaceable. Contrary to what we tend to believe, it is not what we do that makes us who we are but what we want. Desire differentiates. A cow is a cow and one is as good as any other. If my cow fails to do its job, if it stops producing milk, I will go to the cow store and buy myself a new cow. (Admittedly, I know very little about how one acquires a cow.) And, just as one cow can replicate the output of another and thus be used to do the work of its equal, so too are there countless others who can do my job as well as, if not better than, I can. When it comes to work, I can be replaced.

Thus, to define myself as my job is to become one of the herd, a faceless unit in an all-consuming crowd. To find my identity in the work I do is to reject my singularity, to refuse to be what I already am: a multiplicity, an array of desires living and breathing together in one unrepeatable, utterly singular human being. That "our body is but a social structure composed of many souls" is the secret

tive—they would certainly have noticed that Socrates not only admits to corrupting the young and denying the gods of the city, but also to the supposed slanders of studying things in the sky and below the earth and making the worse argument into the stronger. When does he do that? When rebutting the charges of which he actually stands accused, of course. In defending himself against the charge of atheism, he tells us that Meletus' accusation that he, Socrates, thinks "the sun is stone, and the moon earth" is something out of the "books of Anaxagoras" (*Apology*, 26d). But how would one know what those books contain if he has not looked into such matters?[10] What is more, when he refutes the accusation of corrupting the young, he makes a preposterously bad argument—evil is only done out of ignorance—seem stronger than the blatant truth, a truth so obvious that even a child who has yet to reach the age of reason understands it: "It's fun to do bad things."[11]

Now, despite all his feigned ignorance, Socrates understands this too. Indeed, he understands it better than most. But therein lies his ironic cunning. He makes his hearers believe that he does not know and then gets them to look ridiculous by forcing them to either refute his absurd claims or join him in defending them. Either way, they are made to be his dupes, and the laugh is his to enjoy. Might the postmodern teach us to produce so cynical an art? Perhaps. (Though it would demand a kind of self-assurance rarely found in the literary class today.) But in the end, cynicism leads, as indeed the trial of Socrates suggests, to death. It is not generative. It does not create. It is

---

10   Indeed, he even suggests elsewhere that it was not the oracle's riddle but the books of Anaxagoras and his youthful investigation into "what happens to things in the sky and on the earth" that sent him on the philosophical path in the first place. See Plato, *Phaedo*, 96a–100a.

11   The quotation is from a 2008 WPBF 25 News interview with 7-year-old Latarian Milton who, when asked why he stole and crashed his grandmother's SUV, replies: "I wanted to do it 'cause it's fun, it's fun to do bad things and drive a car." https://www.youtube.com/watch?v=qcqOgnQyXp4.

of the philosopher,[28] a secret she must guard and prevent others from finding out. (Hence, the perpetual need in the history of philosophy to *prove* the unity of the soul.) That is because, as Socrates asserts in the *Apology*, philosophy depends upon the *polis*. Without the city structure, the philosopher cannot exist. Society makes desire possible. It allows us to transcend the level of need, to live above brute animal reason. But desire is always the competition of desires, the fight to see who will get to enjoy the fruit of desire[29] and who will be forced to work to make such enjoyment possible for the one who enjoys it. The philosopher is the desirer *par excellence*. She desires knowledge and the power that comes from knowledge, and she can never have enough.

Is it surprising, then, to find philosophers advocating for philosophy and political power to coincide in the same place (*Republic*, 473d)? Is it surprising that Lady Philosophy should declare, "the greatest and most beautiful part of wisdom deals with the proper ordering of cities" (*Symposium*, 209a)? Or might we suggest that if there really is a rift between philosophy and poetry (*Republic*, 607b) it is because the philosopher and the poet are in competition to see who gets to enjoy her manifold desires, and the philosopher, quite shrewdly, has aligned herself with politics, knowing as she does that "politics is the death of art"?[30]

~

Politics is the death of art? Perhaps. Yet in Book VIII, Socrates makes a startling admission. Returning to the question of what role the poets play in his ideal regime, the would-be philosopher king reiterates his earlier claim that most ought to be banished. Now, however, his reason for sending "those children of the gods who have become

---

28 Nietzsche, *Beyond Good and Evil*, §19.
29 Or, alternately, the fruit of *death*, as one charming author recently put it.
30 Beauchard, *The Mask of Memnon*, 35.

How did he go about doing it? By haranguing and harassing his fellow citizens with questions designed to show them that their beliefs were unfounded and that they were actually quite ignorant in spite of the fact that they, like all of us, took themselves to be pretty damned smart. If we accept Socrates at his word and believe that his goal really was to prove his own ignorance, then we must admit he did so masterfully, not knowing that if he tried to publicly demonstrate to another "that he appeared wise to many people and especially to himself, but he was not," that he, Socrates, would be despised and ridiculed and likely put to death (*Apology*, 21c). Did he not know that showing others their folly, especially in front of a troupe of sardonic young scallywags who hung on his every word and were eager to imitate his irksome antics, would make him a pariah? Did he not see that if he continued this practice and refused to give it up, he would be reviled?

Now notice something more. Consider the charges brought against him in court that day. Isn't it odd that in choosing to address the rumors spread about him around Athens, Socrates convicts himself of the very crimes for which he is being tried? Remember, the charges are corrupting the young and not believing in the gods of the city. In confessing his attempt to "refute the oracle" and admitting that he is aware his example inspired brash young men to do the same, did not Socrates condemn himself? But remember, he began his defense by promising to tell the whole truth and not to hide or disguise anything. It is no accident, then, that he openly confesses his guilt. Can he be blamed if his audience refuses to listen? If two and a half millennia worth of readers choose to make themselves the butt of an elaborate joke rather than reading the words printed on the page?

Had his hearers known how to *read*—that is, had they been paying attention as we are now paying attention, rooting out assumptions, catching contradictions, asking questions, in short, reading philosophically, like a detec-

poets" (*Republic*, 366b) into exile has changed. It is no longer because they peddle untruths, but rather because they proclaim the truth too liberally, reveal it to the uninitiated, let the rabble in on the secret wisdom reserved only for the few.

> "It's not for nothing," I said, "that tragedy in general has the reputation of being wise and, within it, Euripides of being particularly so."

> "Why is that?"

> "Because, among other things, he uttered this phrase, the product of shrewd thought, 'tyrants are wise from intercourse with the wise.' And he plainly meant that these men we just spoke of are the wise with whom a tyrant has intercourse."

> "And he and the other poets," he said, "extol tyranny as a condition 'equal to that of a god' and add much else, too."

> "Therefore," I said, "Because the tragic poets are wise, they pardon us, and all those who have regimes resembling ours, for not admitting them into the regime on the ground that they make hymns to tyranny."

> "I suppose," he said, "they pardon us, at least all the subtle ones among them" (*Republic*, 568a–c).

Art, it seems, is the death of politics. For it reveals the nearness of the tyrant and the philosopher, the learned king who becomes wise through intercourse with the wise and the lover of wisdom who desires intercourse for its own sake. Anyone who makes plain the aspirations of the philosopher, who states publicly that the philosopher is on the side of desire and not reason, that the philosopher is the desirer *par excellence*, is liable to expulsion. And rightly so. For it is to the advantage of the philosopher to be able to "soothe and gently persuade" (*Republic*, 476e) those who are sick with desire that health resides in the letting go of desire, that wellbeing can only be achieved by renounc-

mer is sardonic, contemptuous, its humor hinging on the (admittedly warranted) debasement of others. The latter is light, mirthful, it invites readers to laugh along as initiates to the mysteries of an inside joke.

Let us look closer. The *Apology*, you will remember, begins with Socrates' insistence that in order to address the charges brought against him—corrupting the young and not believing in the gods of the city—he must first confront the rumors that have been circulating among his fellow Athenians, namely, that "Socrates is guilty of wrongdoing in that he busies himself studying things in the sky and below the earth; he makes the worse into the stronger argument, and he teaches these same things to others" (*Apology*, 19b–c). Now pay attention to how he rebuts these so-called "first accusers." His defense runs as follows: One day, Chaerephon—Socrates' closest companion, so close in fact that Donne penned *The Flea* in honor of them[9]—set off for Delphi to ask of the oracle the only question on anyone's mind. *Who is the wisest man in Athens, and why is it Socrates?* Knowing Socrates' affinity for playing the flute, his propensity for going catatonic, and his ability to drink even the most illustrious of drinkers "under the table," the oracle quite naturally confused him with a statue of Silenus (see, *Symposium*, 215b; 220c–d; and 220a, respectively). This, the god must have thought, would make for a fine joke—to say that the pinnacle of Athenian wisdom could be found in a hollow statue. After all, what better way to convey "that human wisdom is worth little or nothing" than to make of it an elaborate joke (*Apology*, 23a)? The problem was that Socrates, fashioning himself the new Oedipus, took the joke not as a joke but as a riddle and thought he might even lift the plague of human ignorance from his city if only he could solve it. And so, he set off to "refute the oracle" by finding someone wiser than himself so he could say, "This man is wiser than I, but you said I was" (*Apology*, 21b).

---

9   Cf. Aristophanes, *The Clouds*, lines 144–147.

ing that which makes them human. After all, not everyone can enjoy his humanity to the same degree. The pursuit of desire is a war over who gets to pursue his desire. And if that insatiable pursuit is reserved only for the few, then it is up to those few to make sure that others know nothing of it. How then can the philosopher not resent the poet, the one who reveals the philosopher's deceit?

Well, not every poet reveals the philosopher's deceit. There are, as Adeimantus observes, a subtle few—rare, to be sure—who see the benefit of the deception and learn to play the game. There are those who know the most beautiful dithyrambs are sung through the mask of justice (cf. *Republic*, 361a). But where to find such subtle poets? Where the clever imitators composing their hymns to Apollo? Where—if not hidden in works of philosophy? For, it is the rare artistic genius who understands that the pleasure of the greatest jokes resides in the fact that few people get them. And where better for the playful philosopher-poet to hide himself and have his fun than in a book whose intended audience has proved time and again to be "the source of laughter" for many (*Republic*, 517a), whose readers have earned a "reputation of buffoonery" (*Republic*, 606c) in spite of their red-faced insistence that philosophic "truth must be taken seriously" (*Republic*, 389b)? Why not end the "old quarrel between philosophy and poetry" (*Republic*, 607b) by making the philosopher the unwitting butt of an inside joke (cf. *Republic*, 396d)?

An example will help to illustrate the point. One would expect readers to be wary of an author who publishes under multiple names. Yet that Kierkegaard, master of Socratic irony and poetic misdirection, might offer an argument in jest is a gag too obvious for most readers to get. Take the following passage from *Fear and Trembling*:

If a human being did not have an eternal consciousness, if

before them, whereas we beat our heads against it. They were free enough to admire and be charmed by their own making, whereas we make nothing and confine ourselves to the role of critic, arching an ironic eyebrow and apologizing self-consciously after every cynical remark. Yes, if life in the cave is harsh, we have made it harsher and have grown more discontented thereby. We call ourselves enlightened, but our enlightenment amounts to nothing more than acknowledging what our ancestors knew (and knew better than us) and then foreswearing their consolations. If we have struggled to get beyond the postmodern—and this, I believe, is the least contentious point made in this humble little book—that is because the postmodern is a method of critique. It affirms nothing. It is, to use Nietzsche's nomenclature, a product of *ressentiment*. It aims to demolish what's come before but offers no vision of what might come next.

Well, not no vision perhaps. If we postmoderns have been willing to learn any lesson from the past, it is that Socratic irony grounds Platonic artistry, though we have yet to make the move from irony to art. In part, that is because, for all its pretenses, the postmodern is an embarrassingly earnest movement, one too pained by the hypocrisy of the world to delight in it. (Fredric Jameson's characterization of postmodernism as "the substitute for the sixties and the compensation for their political failure" nods at the disillusioned utopianism that undergirds our epoch to this day.)[8] More than anything, however, it is because Socratism (that is, irony) never lets go of the self, whereas art demands abandon. Take two more examples from the dialogues before we leave them behind. First, Socrates' ironical self-defense in the *Apology*. Second, his aesthetically sophisticated second speech on love in the *Phaedrus*. Both evince the kind of levity with language that only an author who has seen through the social veneer and found veneer hiding underneath is free enough to produce. Yet the for-

---

8   Jameson, *Postmodernism, or, The Cultural Logic of Late Capitalism*, xvi.

underlying everything there were only a wild, fermenting power that writhing in dark passions produced everything, be it significant or insignificant, if a vast, never appeased emptiness hid beneath everything, what would life be then but despair? If such were the situation, if there were no sacred bond that knit humankind together, if one generation emerged after another like forest foliage, if one generation succeeded another like the singing of birds in the forest, if a generation passed through the world as a ship through the sea, as wind through the desert, an unthinking and unproductive performance, if an eternal oblivion, perpetually hungry, lurked for its prey and there were no power strong enough to wrench that away from it—how empty and devoid of consolation life would be! But precisely for this reason it is not so . . .[31]

Now the typical reader of philosophy, being a member of the world's most humorless lot, fails to see beneath the surface of a text like this and thus takes its author at his word. (Kierkegaard, after all, is a Christian, and no Christian could believe in a bleak and meaningless world bordering on nonexistence and perpetual dark.)[32] Taking for granted the sincerity of this philosophical word-wizard, the reader goes on to accept the distinction offered in the pages that follow between the poet and the hero, the one who writes and the one who fights, and in so doing, misses the punchline and misreads the text. What such readers fail to grasp is that Kierkegaard's knight of faith—like the errant knight Don Quixote, after whom he is modeled—is both hero and poet, Cervantes to himself, author of his deeds, one who lives out the adventures he writes with the story of his life. And failing to understand that, they fail to understand the philosophy altogether.

Similarly, the jokes of Plato are missed by the many and perhaps even the few who don't know that the joke is on them. Returning once more to the banishment of the poets, consider the style of writing Socrates finds most repugnant:

---

31   Kierkegaard, *Fear and Trembling*, 15.
32   Cf. Augustine, *Confessions*, (12.7.7).

images (that is, artifice) invented to give the semblance of structure to a world that otherwise overwhelms us. Beneath them is—what? Chaos? The noumenal? Prime matter? The Lacanian real? The animus mundi? Who knows. The point is the construction, the unreality we take to be real.

This is all pretty standard stuff, or at least it seems to be, until one asks: *Why the cave?* Why depict man as learning to think and speak and understand in terms of images inked on stone? What image does the image suggest? Two come readily to mind. The first is the tomb. Life as we live it is a kind of inclosure, a straitjacket that fixes us in our place as the grave fixes the immovable dead. (That the God of the Christians is both born and buried in a cave is a point too suggestive to go unmentioned here.) The second is the dwelling place of our caveman ancestors, beyond whom we have hardly progressed. As I've suggested already, if the postmodern has been good for anything—and, indeed, it has been good for much—it is showing us that our world, like theirs, is a world built upon power, a world of unknowing and belief in which superstition prevails because the darkness is too dark to face and we live in constant fear of what we cannot master, a world in which meaning and certainty resist us and we must content ourselves with the artifacts we create or risk plunging headlong into the misery and discontent that arise from an honest confrontation with the rock, the wall of our prison, the unchanging edifice arching before us. That rock is, as Dostoevsky's underground man says, a stone wall, an insurmountable barrier between man and his desires, an image of the impossibility and futility of human affairs.

What is one to do with so plain and pitiless a fact? Where turn when one's home is set against him? The answer, of course, is nothing and nowhere—though you could spruce the walls up a bit with a few strokes of wet paint. This is the genius of our cave-dwelling ancestors and the stumbling block of postmodern man. For they were content to decorate (and thus transform) the obstacle

"when someone takes out the poet's connections between the speeches and leaves the exchanges" (*Republic*, 394b)— that is, dialogue. But not just any kind of dialogue; the kind that "proceeds wholly by imitation" (*Republic*, 394c)—that is, fictional dialogue. Especially fictional dialogue that brings together "two kinds of imitation that seem close to one another, like writing comedy and tragedy . . . at the same time" (*Republic*, 395a)—that is, the fictional dialogues of Plato (see *Symposium*, 223d). And what is worse? Fictional dialogues that depict such shameful things as a woman "who's abusing her husband" (*Republic*, 395d; cf. *Phaedo*, 60a); or "one who's caught in the grip of misfortune, mourning and wailing" (*Republic*, 395e; cf. *Phaedo*, 117d–e); or "one who's striving with the gods and boasting because she supposes herself happy" (*Republic*, 395d–e; cf. *Symposium*, 203b–212c); or "one who's sick or in love or in labor" (*Republic*, 395e; cf. *Symposium*, 206a–208b). And of course, no true poet would "imitate slaves" (*Republic*, 395e; cf. *Meno* 82b–85b).

> Nor, as it seems, bad men [cf. Alcibiades, Charmides, Critias, Meno, etc.] who are cowards and . . . insulting and making fun of one another [cf. Socrates' conversations with Thrasymachus, Callicles, etc.] and using shameful language [cf. *Gorgias* 494e to cite the first instance that comes to mind], drunk or sober [cf. *Symposium*, 212e], or committing the other faults that such men commit against themselves and others in speeches and deeds. Nor do I suppose they should be accustomed to likening themselves to madmen in speeches or in deeds [cf. *Symposium*, 173e; *Phaedrus*, 244a–245c]. For, although they must know both mad and worthless men and women, they must neither do nor imitate anything of theirs (*Republic*, 395e–396a).

The works of Plato, in short, would be banned in Socrates' proposed *polis* and their author sent "to another city" (*Republic*, 398a). For, although such a subtle poet—"able by wisdom to become every sort of thing and to imitate all things"—is "a man sacred, wonderful, and pleasing"

The postmodern helps us to see that behind every shadow is a world of shadows. It takes seriously Nietzsche's claim that each mask only conceals another mask and that, as *personae*, we are all masked actors, fictional characters playing various parts on life's dramatic stage.

Yet is this an accurate depiction of existence in the cave? Are we merely revelers dancing for no one in some sad theatre of the absurd? To answer this, we must attend to the image and what the shadows that flicker across the stoney walls depict. Let us return, then, to Plato, metarealist *par excellence*, and see how he, as the worn-out dictum of Carl Dreyer would have it, uses artifice to strip artifice of artifice. Socrates, Plato's most renowned, though certainly not his noblest, invention[7] begins his work of fiction by presenting us with a herd of prisoners, shackled in place, eyes fixed firmly on the rock before them. Restrained and thus unable to turn their heads, they spend their days discussing shadows produced by other human beings who parade "artifacts" (Socrates' word) in front of a fire in order to deceive them with projections, "statues of men and other animals wrought from stone, wood and every kind of material" (*Republic*, 514c).

Such artifacts are, of course, "artificial things" (*Republic*, 515c), constructs molded by human hands. But so too are the shadows and thus the foundations of thought. We think, the image suggests, in images. Further, we rely upon manmade concepts—measure, number, shape, time, space, etc.—in order to differentiate one image from another and delineate each as a separate being. Those concepts too are

---

proaches that are keen on criticizing others but refuse to undergo that most essential of philosophical critiques, self-examination. Those who truck with ideologies that claim to "expose" or "uncover" the supposedly true foundations of a given worldview yet never interrogate the truth of that truth have less to do with philosophy than the sophists of Athens.

7　That honor, I'm afraid, belongs to the one whom he fittingly dubs "beautiful immortal glory"—though, of course, few readers of Plato are subtle enough to perceive what the name suggests. (I'm indebted to a friend called Lucian for drawing this to my attention.)

(*Republic*, 398a), so too is he an all-various man, an insatiable desirer, and thus a threat to the social order. He is, upon closer examination, a tyrant. A "manifold" (*Republic*, 588e), "many-headed" (*Republic*, 589a), "many-formed beast" (*Republic*, 590a). He is "*Eros* incarnate" as Strauss calls him.[33] A wolf who is ready to cull his own.

And yet, this is Plato's great joke—that no one knows it.[34] Rather, he "seems to have discovered an art which he has disguised very well" (*Phaedrus*, 273c). For he is "such an artful speaker," so able to "escape detection" as he shifts "from one thing to its opposite," that he can "toy with his audience and mislead them" (*Phaedrus*, 261d–262d), say one thing to "those with understanding" and another to "those who have no business" reading his works (*Phaedrus*, 275e), earn for himself "immortal fame as a speech writer" (*Phaedrus*, 258c), make himself "equal to the gods while he is still alive" and convince "those who live in later times [to] believe the same about him when they behold his writings" (*Phaedrus*, 258c). Contrary to Strauss's insistence that the poets are banished from the *Republic* because "philosophy as quest for truth is the highest activity of man and poetry is not concerned with truth,"[35] we now find that the philosopher-tyrant expels the poets with his art. His art is his justice, to borrow another line from Strauss, because if justice is doing one job and minding one's business (cf. *Republic*, 433a), and the philosopher-poet's job is "to become every sort of thing and to imitate all things" (*Republic*, 398a) while at the same time "tast[ing] every kind of learning with gusto" (*Republic*, 475c) and organizing and leading a city (*Republic*, 474c)—that is, doing every job and minding everyone's business—then the philosopher-poet-tyrant-king becomes just precisely by being

---

33 Strauss, *The City and Man*, 133.
34 Well, maybe not no one. See Beauchard's charming little blog post, "The Appearance of Justice: Three Philosophical Villains Unmasked," which appeared in the Montreal Review in October of 2023.
35 Strauss, *The City and Man*, 134.

church and act as if it were no amputation. True enough. And yet, we live in a post-Enlightenment age. The two have already been put asunder. (And what man hath separated, let no god join together again.) Nowhere is this more evident than in the treatment of human remains. In the United States, for example, unclaimed bodies are typically cremated by the state. The ashes are held for a time then scattered or interred. The names of the dead are logged in official registers and their deaths tallied alongside those who comprise the most unhappy of statistics. The church, on the other hand, insists upon burying its dead. It erects monuments and commemorates the entombed with prayers, holy days, festivals, and incantations. In doing so, it admits what's been lost and seeks to resurrect it through art. *Art, you say? Can the word be stretched to include this?* Yes, art. For what else would you call the transfiguration through song, story, meal, memory, and chant of trauma into tragedy, tragedy into celebration, celebration into jubilation—the resurrection of the dead?

Leaving aside questions of transcendence, we encounter here, on purely secular grounds, a first gesture at that which will get us beyond the postmodern. I said above that the questions posed by an honest consideration of the cave are whether we've actually understood the shadows—what they are and what they are meant to divert us from—and, assuming we have, how we ought to proceed. The postmodern, it would seem, opens for us the possibility of addressing the former. It offers no assistance, however, with the latter—please feel free to disregard the theatrical guffaws coming from those last decrepit deconstructionists lingering in the back—and, as my "it would seem" was meant to suggest, we oughtn't be too quick to accept its assessment of either. What is helpful about the postmodern disposition is that, as a method of critique, it is unwilling to accept answers and remains instead with questions.[6]

---

[6]   This, at least, is what it is meant to do in its more honest forms. True philosophers have little patience for the so-called critical ap-

unjust and replacing the artists, the lawgivers, the priests, the statesmen with himself.

To put it most simply, such a man is a greater artist than his rivals, capable of making "everyone who has ever attempted to compose a speech seem like a child in comparison" (*Phaedrus*, 279a). And yet with time, he comes to see his own writing as beneath him, a means of "amusing himself" and nothing more (*Phaedrus*, 276d). With his pen, he outdoes his competition, undermines their authority, damages their reputations (see *Apology*, 21b–23a; *Republic*, 599b–601a; *Symposium*, 199d–201c; and so on). He continues to do so "until he purges the city" of their presence (*Republic*, 567c) and crowns himself the victor (cf. *Symposium*, 213e). But he doesn't stop there. "A higher, divine impulse leads him to more important things" (*Phaedrus*, 279a). That impulse is called *desire*. And those strivings will form in him a new and noble ideal, the creation of a previously unimagined art, an art that points us, if we let it, beyond the postmodern, toward that which creates the world anew (cf. *Letter II*, 314c; *Cratylus*, 432b–c).[36]

---

36   See, Beauchard, "Who it the Philosopher King?," 277–282.

be funny if it wasn't so tragic. The ramifications are everywhere on display. Belligerence is celebrated in the public square. Confusion spreads like pestilence across the land. The Asclepiads of old, those subtle doctors and healers of the human condition, are nowhere to be found. Today, man fashions himself wise and is more ignorant than ever. Today, the learned are as foppish as the fops, and none have read enough to know the difference. What can be done when the blind are content to be led by the blind? Where go when no one comprehends where he is? The cave seems like a place to start. For, if it is true that the postmodern is about revealing the shadows as shadows, if it's meant to bring us down into the depths and go deeper still, excavating what's hidden beneath what's hidden beneath, then we'll have to begin by asking ourselves, first, if we've really understood what's been laid bare, and second, supposing we have, what are we to do with so tragic a vision?

Tragic, you say? Why tragic? Must the foundations conceal something monstrous? Man buries corpses, that's true enough. But so too is he known to bury treasure. Might not a hidden mirth, a mysterious merriment, reside at the heart of all things? No, I think not. Or at least not if we take the cave as our starting point. For, the cave is the city of man and there can be no denying that "our cities are erected atop burial grounds."[5] So too, one might argue, are our churches—a fact which ought not to be glibly dismissed. But while the former devise means of diverting us from the burial of the dead, the latter build belltowers to proclaim it. This is a stark contrast. Civilization distracts and, to the degree to which it can, protects us from mortality. The church—with its incessant *now and at the hour of our death*s and *to dust you shall returns*—thrusts it before us. Which ought the philosopher to prefer?

The dichotomy, you will say, is a false one. Only a post-Enlightenment thinker would cleave the city from the

---

5   Beauchard, *City of Man*, xiii.

Bibliography[37]

Aristophanes, *Lysistrata and Other Plays*, trans. Alan H. Sommerstein (London, UK: Penguin Books, 2003).

Aristotle, *Poetics*, trans. Anthony Kenny (Oxford, UK: Oxford University Press, 2013).

Augustine, *Confessions*, trans. Maria Boulding (New York, NY: Vintage, 1998).

Auster, Paul, *City of Glass* (New York, NY: Penguin Publishing Group, 1987).

Beauchard, Jean-Luc, *City of Man: A Novel Reading of Plato's Republic* (Eugune, OR: Cascade Books, 2023).

Beauchard, Jean-Luc, "Who is the Philosopher King?," in *misReading Plato: Continental and Psychoanalytic Glimpses Beyond the Mask*, eds. Matthew Clemente, Bryan Cocchiara, and William Hendel (London, UK: Routledge, 2022).

Borges, Jorge Luis, *Collected Fictions*, trans. Andrew Hurley (New York, NY: Penguin Publishing Group, 1999).

Brown, Norman, *Life Against Death: The Psychoanalytical Meaning of History* (Middletown, CT: Wesleyan University Press, 1985).

Burnett, D. Graham, Catherine L. Hansen, and Justin E. H. Smith, *In Search of The Third Bird: Exemplary Essays from The Proceedings of ESTAR(SER), 2001–2021.* (Boston, MA: MIT Press, 2021).

---

37 Incomplete and possibly inaccurate, mostly from laziness and lack of scholarly rigor, but partly from assumed license to throw off "petty academic conventions."

sary? Yes and no. To be sure, one must upend one's father if one is to get out from under the old man's shadow. But he's not the only one who deserves a good drubbing. No, if what we have said about being born in tradition is true, and it is equally true that to undermine one's inheritance is the meanest form of ingratitude, then the philosophic patricide is left to ask—*Why tradition? What good is gratitude?* The philosopher knows no sacred cow. (The nonphilosopher, on the other hand, is marked by an enthusiasm for worship.) It is only by getting to the root, by razing even the foundations and probing around underneath, that one becomes a philosopher. It is only when the idols before which so many have fallen are smashed that one finds a few things worth saying. But what can be said about what lies beneath? What language is left to him who dismantles language? There can be no doubt: The language of philosophy. That is, the language of tradition.

How now? Are we to return to the old tyrant's doorstep and ask to be welcomed in? Are we to play prodigal son and come, hat in hand, begging for our cell back? Is *this* what it means to get beyond the postmodern? Not at all. Once the shadows on the wall of the cave have been seen for what they are, they won't be seen as anything else. Disillusion is loss. Naïveté cannot be recaptured. When one is a child, one is content to think like a child. But when one grows old, the time has come to put childish thoughts away. Meaning? Objectivity? Free will? Justice? These are the vestiges of infantile illusions. They crumble under the least scrutiny. And yet, so too do their postpostmodern alternatives. Having deposed the ideals of the past, we've found no successors to set upon their thrones. We tout our progress. We champion our reason. But after toppling the temple, all we can do is stand in the ruins and call it the New Jerusalem.

Is there anyone who doubts that this is no New Jerusalem? Is there anyone whose life is not dogged by some profound discontent? Today's unmoored quixotism would

Burnett, D. G., Dolven, J., Hansen, C. L., and Smith, J. E. H.,
    "Metafiction and the Study of History: Makerly Knowledge
    in the Archive," *Rethinking History* 27, no. 3 (2023): 537–557.

Camus, Albert, *The Myth of Sisyphus*, trans. Justin O'Brien (New
    York, NY: Vintage, 1991).

Camus, Albert, *Les Cahiers de la Pléiade*, trans. Sandra Smith,
    <https://www.penguin.co.uk/articles/2020/may/albert-
    camus-the-plague-an-appeal-to doctors.html>.

Cervantes, Miguel, *Don Quixote*, trans. John Rutherford (Lon-
    don, UK, Penguin Publishing Group, 2003).

Clemente, Matthew, *Eros Crucified: Death, Desire, and the Divine
    in Psychoanalysis and Philosophy of Religion* (London, UK:
    Routledge, 2019).

Clemente, Matthew, "The Folly of Morychus," in *Metarealism
    and the Future of Art: Bacchus Agonistes* (Boston, MA: Senex
    Press, 2024).

Clemente, Matthew, "Touch Thyself: Kearney's Anacarnational
    Return to Plato's Forgotten Wisdom," in *Anacarnation*, eds.
    Brian Treanor and James Taylor (London, UK: Routledge,
    2023).

Dostoevsky, Fyodor, *Notes From Underground*, trans. Jessie Coul-
    son (New York, NY: Penguin, 1972).

Dostoevsky, Fyodor, *The Idiot*, trans. Richard Pevear and Larissa
    Volokhonsky (Vintage Classics, 2003).

Emerson, Ralph Waldo, *Self-Reliance and Other Essays* (Nash-
    ville, TN: American Renaissance Books, 2010).

Erasmus, Desiderius, *The Praise of Folly: Updated Edition*, trans.
    Anthony Grafton (Princeton, NJ: Princeton University
    Press, 2015).

Feyerabend, Paul, *Against Method* (New York, NY. Verso Books,
    2010).

one follows that logic far enough, if one pushes down the path of regress and refuses to stop, one finds it to be as infinite as the stars. *Quod est absurdum!* replies the bowtied logician with chalk dust on his lapel. (In response to this, one can only smile.) Yes, the regress is infinite, and it is impenetrable, the way back as opaque as the way ahead. And yet, one must begin. How then to proceed?

This *How then—*, it should be clear, is the fundamental problem of philosophy. It is a problem one answers not by answering but by doing, a challenge that must be confronted with action, a question to which the practice of philosophy is the only fitting answer. Note that I say the *practice* of philosophy, not a given philosophy or philosophical system. To philosophize, to be a philosopher, is already to stake a claim. It is to assert a right, an authority to which few are privileged. But that right comes at a cost. There are always tradeoffs in this world, and no one puts bread into his belly without depriving the belly of another. Whose sustenance do I consume when I claim for myself the mantle of wisdom's lover? In a recent work which offers much to criticize and much to commend, the highly original political theorist Jean-Luc Beauchard writes, "the philosopher is born of patricide, born of the recognition that freedom comes from questioning everything—especially the authority, laws, and customs of the father (including that most demanding of fathers, the state)."[3] That the wise and glorious Sophocles should live up to his name by gifting us the first philosopher king, a ruler capable of plumbing the depths of human nature but struggling to know himself, is perhaps fitting. After all, the poets are always revealing the tragedy of striving for "godlike power over others," and there can be no greater embodiment of that despotic spirit than Oedipus tyrannus.[4]

What? Freud was right after all? The patricidal lust is not only irresistible—for some natures, it is even neces-

---

3　Beauchard, *City of Man*, 85.
4　Euripides, *The Trojan Women*, line 1169. Cf. Plato, *Republic*, 568b.

Freud, Sigmund, *Civilization and Its Discontents*, trans. James Strachey (New York, NY: W. W. Norton, 1962).

Freud, Sigmund, *Introductory Lectures on Psychoanalysis*, trans. James Strachey (New York, NY: W. W. Norton, 1977).

Jameson, Fredric, *Postmodernism, or, The Cultural Logic of Late Capitalism* (Durham, NC: Duke University Press, 1991).

Kearney, Richard, "As If It Were True: An Interview with Matthew Clemente," in *The Los Angeles Review of Books*. June 21, 2020, <https://lareviewofbooks.org/article/ as-if-it-were-true-an-interview-with-richard-kearney/>.

Kearney, Richard, "The Philosophical Poet and the Poetic Philosopher: Matthew Clemente in Dialogue with Richard Kearney," in *misReading Plato: Continental and Psychoanalytic Glimpses Beyond the Mask*, eds. Matthew Clemente, Bryan Cocchiara, and William Hendel (London, UK: Routledge, 2022).

Kierkegaard, Søren, *Fear and Trembling*, trans. Howard Hong and Edna Hong (Princeton, NJ: Princeton University Press, 1983).

Kierkegaard, Søren, *The Sickness unto Death*, trans. Howard Hong and Edna Hong (Princeton, NJ: Princeton University Press, 1983).

Lyotard, Jean-Francois, *The Postmodern Condition: A Report on Knowledge*, trans. Brian Massumi and Geoffrey Bennington (Minneapolis, MN: University of Minnesota Press, 1984).

Madrox, J. P., *The Philosopher King: A Novel* (Eugune, OR: Cascade Books, 2024).

Montaigne, Michel, *An Apology for Raymond Sebond*, trans. M. A. Screech (London, UK: Penguin Books Limited, 2006).

Nietzsche, Friedrich, *Beyond Good and Evil*, trans. Walter Kaufmann (New York, NY: Vintage, 1989).

upon others and thus must ingratiate ourselves to others if we hope to survive. Conformity is no mean thing. It is the law. It represents, in its essence, a wish to live, a desire to carry on and even, perhaps, to flourish. This is as true of peoples as it is of persons. Societies survive by likening themselves to their predecessors, modeling their cultures and systems of government on the successes of the past. Every period of advancement is also a renaissance, every revolution, a revival. Is it an accident that the heights of human achievement continue to harken back to Athens? No more of an accident, surely, than the Athenians' emulation of the triumphs of Egypt, a civilization which was already ancient in the ancient world. What has been will be again, as the good book says, and what will be already is. Originality is as impudent as it is impossible. Impudent because innovation masks decadence, a self-indulgent dampening of the past that leads to a repetition of past failures already overcome. Impossible because no one can divorce himself from the accident of his birth. We are born in the running waters of tradition, and though we may swim against or even attempt to divert the stream, we can never escape its flow.

The philosopher understands this better than most, the philosopher whose sole job is recollection. To *re*-member, to collect the fragments of the past, of what has been and is no more, and assemble them into an image at once familiar and striking—is this not the task every philosopher has before him? But where to begin? How to shore up a vision of what was against the tides of time such that the current can be channeled into a fertile future? Knowledge of the tradition is not enough. It must become one's daily bread. One must take it into oneself and make it into oneself and—it must be said—excrete whatever offers no nutritional value. One begins simply enough. There are various schools, and one desires to know them. But in order to understand any system of thought, one must understand the system it refutes. That's a maxim. The problem is, if

Nietzsche, Friedrich, *The Birth of Tragedy from the Spirit of Music*, trans. Walter Kaufmann (New York, NY: Vintage, 1967).

Plato, *Charmides*, trans. Christopher Moore and Christopher Raymond (Indianapolis, IN: Hackett, 2019).

Plato, *The Republic of Plato*, trans. Allan Bloom (New York, NY: Basic Books, 2016).

Plato, *Symposium*, trans. Alexander Nehamas and Paul Woodruff (Indianapolis, IN: Hackett, 1989).

Plato, *Phaedrus*, trans. Alexander Nehamas and Paul Woodruff (Indianapolis, IN: Hackett, 1989).

Plato, *Momucles* in *Complete Works*, trans. Joaquim Maria Nivola, ed. John M. Cooper. (Indianapolis, IN: Hackett, 1997) 971–1223.

Plato, *Five Dialogues: Euthyphro, Apology, Crito, Meno, Phaedo*, trans. G. M. A. Grube (Indianapolis, IN: Hackett, 2002).

Rugg, Richmond, *The Wisdom of Silenus: A Commentary on Plato's Momucles*, vols. I–IV (Carbunk, MA: Fenwick University Press, 1981).

Sartre, Jean-Paul, *Being and Nothingness: An Essay on Phenomenological Ontology*, trans. Hazel Bames (New York, NY: Simon and Schuster, 1992).

Strauss, Leo, *The City and Man* (Chicago, IL: University of Chicago Press, 1978).

Unamuno, Miguel, *Fog: A Novel*, trans. Alberto Manguel (Evanston, IL: Northwestern University Press, 2017).

Wilde, Oscar, *The Decay of Lying: And Other Essays* (London, UK: Penguin Publishing Group, 2021).

The Folly of Morychus

"This art of theirs seems to me something marvelous and lofty. . . . it is a part of the enchanters' art and but slightly inferior to it."

~ *Euthydemus*, 289e

In a recent essay which bore as its subtitle "Beyond the Postmodern,"[1] I opened with a bit of a riff on Emerson's "The American Scholar" that was really a veiled critique of "Self-Reliance." The title of the present book is a rather obvious allusion to an unfinished play by TS Eliot. Allow me, then, to take the opportunity to subtly undermine Eliot's central claim in another, apparently disrelated text.[2] Doing so will, I hope, shine some light upon the difficulty posed by the postmodern posture of suspicion, irony, and critique. The postmodern is, after all, fundamentally tied to the modern, and Eliot is the archmodernist. Let us then take up the question of tradition's relation to the individual philosopher and how, after the artistic structure of western culture has been leveled stone by stone until the foundations on which it rests have become visible, it is now possible to erect something new.

It is not blasphemous, I take it, to acknowledge that the need to be like others, the need to be *liked* by others, is one of the most basic human needs. Donne's sacred truism "No man is an island" amounts to acknowledging the contingency of our being, the inescapable fact that we depend

---

1   The essay referred to is the first essay in this book, originally published under the title "The Multiplicity of Man: Beyond the Postmodern."

2   No, not *The Waste Land*, in which, we must simply admit, the poet tackled a problem that proved too much for him. Why he attempted it at all is an insoluble puzzle; under compulsion of what experience he attempted to express the inexpressibly horrible, we cannot ever know.

Contents

"And neither Pindar, nor Aeschylus, nor Hesiod, nor Homer, nor any of the greater poets or teachers of any nation or time, ever spoke but with intentional reservation ..."

~ John Ruskin, *The Queen of Air: Being a Study of the Greek Myths of Cloud and Storm*

An Homage to JC
No more, Pomona, let thy vot'ries chaunt
The praise of Cyder; no, nor Ceres bring
Her grain for beery clowns. Avaunt, avaunt!
Bacchus is our undoubted Lord and King!

Metarealism and the Future of Art
Bacchus Agonistes

by Matthew Clemente

SENEX
PRESS

Metarealism and the Future of Art

www.ingramcontent.com/pod-product-compliance
Lightning Source LLC
Chambersburg PA
CBHW061547310726
48972CB00008B/2654